PRIVATE MESSAGES

KELLY CHEEK

Cover and book design by Kelly Cheek

ISBN: 978-1-7335022-1-4

Fiery Muse Publishing
Littleton, Colorado 80129

Printed in the United States of America

Parker Sage tried not to be distracted by the trickle of sweat he felt snaking its way down his back. Keeping the trigger depressed, he tapped the nail gun in a descending pattern down the end 2x4, joining it to the one on the wall they had stood just a little while before, creating a sturdy corner post. As he stepped back, Joe and Bud started bolting down the bottom plate of the new framed wall to the foundation. Parker turned away, dragging the nail gun's hose away from where they were working, but not before noticing the cold look that Bud shot toward him.

Parker put the nail gun down near the compressor just as it stopped chugging. It was the end of a hot day in August, and he wiped sweat from his eyebrows just before it rolled down into his eyes. He leaned against a couple of studs and looked out at the new subdivision. Hickory Creek, just north of Raleigh, North Carolina, had several houses completed, and a few were even occupied. But for the most part, the subdivision was still a work in progress. Streets had been scraped through the wooded area, some paved, some still just dirt.

Down the street, a cement crew was busy cleaning their tools. A foundation had been poured that morning, and they had spent a good portion of the day finishing its surface. That's the house that Parker and his crew were scheduled to start framing next.

If they didn't kill each other before then.

"I know you've been fucking her, man!" Bud said. Parker sighed and turned around.

Bud was standing there holding the socket wrench he had just used to tighten the bolts on the bottom plate of the new wall. He was gripping it like a weapon, but its diminutive size almost made Parker smile.

Almost.

"Bud, come on, man," he said quietly, calmly. "I swear to you, I've never been with Shelly. Not like that."

It was an accusation Parker had heard before, but before, it had been more of a joke than a real accusation. Bud's wife was a notorious flirt, and Bud was pretty sure she was cheating on him.

Pretty much anybody who knew her thought so.

"I love my *own* wife," Parker continued. "Why would I want yours?"

"Well, maybe because *your* wife is a downer!" Bud shot back, a vein in his temple standing out sharply. "You got yourself a really fucked up woman, man. And it makes sense she's so unhappy. She's married to you!"

"Bud, you little shit, Lily's depressed," Parker said, feeling an emotional fatigue settle over him. "I've told you this before. Talk like that about her again and I'll kick your ass."

Bud didn't respond. Joe watched awkwardly from a few feet away, not sure what to do or say. In that moment of Bud's hesitation, Parker continued.

"Look, Bud, I know you're suspicious about Shelly. Hell, we are too. After hearing some of the shit you've told us, I'm *certain* she's having an affair. But how can you think it's me? What makes you think *I'd* do that? I'm your friend, man. We've known each other since second grade."

"She's always talking about how good looking you are," Bud said reluctantly. "She feels sorry for you because you got such a fucked up wife, and says you need someone who can take care of you."

"Shit, Bud, that's it?" Parker asked incredulously.

"Bud," Joe finally spoke up, "you and I have said that too. I mean look at him. The son of a bitch is built like a goddamn Greek god! We've both commented on what a good looking guy he is. Doesn't mean *you're* getting it on with Parker. I know *I'm* not."

Parker smiled with deepening dimples, and Bud, against his will, felt his resolve beginning to crack. In an effort to hold on to it, he continued.

"She was going on last night about how, if she was married to you, she'd make sure you were always happy and satisfied, 'cause you deserve it."

"Well I can't argue with that," Parker said with a slight smile. "I do deserve it. But I'm not screwing your wife, man. I wouldn't do that to you."

Bud shifted back and forth a couple of times, mentally processing what Parker said, before he sighed.

"I know," he said. Parker noticed that Bud's grip relaxed on the socket wrench. "She just gets me so worked up, I feel like I need to punch somebody!"

"Well, just as long as it's not me," Parker said, now with a full smile.

"Yeah, right," Bud said with an embarrassed tone. "Your arms are as big as my thighs. It'd probably be the last punch I ever threw. You'd kill me."

"Come on, buddy, you're my friend. I couldn't kill you. Break your arms, maybe." In spite of himself, Bud smiled. Parker took a couple of steps toward Bud with his hand outstretched. Bud sighed and put the socket wrench in a pouch on his tool belt, then shook Parker's hand.

"Damn, Bud," Joe said, "you said she was talking about that last night. What made you wait till the end of today to get all worked up about it?"

Bud sighed again and shook his head.

"At lunch, I read a text message that Shelly sent me. I mean it was nothing, but in the text, she also asked how Parker was. After last night, that pissed me off. Then a little while ago, I saw that pretty little filly next door ogling Parker." All three of them unconsciously glanced toward the house. Numerous times, they had noticed the young blonde watching from her window, usually keeping to the shadows. "Well, on top of the shit with Shelly, I just got mad. I'm sorry, Park. I didn't mean any of that."

"Don't worry about it," Parker said with a shake of his head. He looked toward the wall they had just stood. "You guys get a brace on the end of that wall. I'll roll up the hoses and we can go get a beer."

They all nodded, and as Bud and Joe turned back toward the new wall, Parker took off his tool belt and headed toward his black Silverado extended cab pickup. He gathered up the nail guns and put them in the tool box in the back of his truck, then rolled up the air hoses. Within a few minutes time, Bud and Joe joined him with other tools and the electrical cords.

The day had been hot and humid, and Parker had left his shirt draped over the 2x4s stacked on the south side of the house they were currently working on. He went to retrieve his shirt, which took him near the house next door, one that was now occupied. By the good looking young blonde who just happened to be watching him from the window.

He smiled and waved, but she backed up away from the window, back into the shadows. He snorted as he picked up his shirt. He was sweaty from the hot day's work, so it was a bit of a struggle to pull the shirt on. But he purposely emphasized the struggle in order to flex his muscles even more than was necessary. He glanced back up at the window and saw that she was still there, and had, in fact, moved closer to the window again as she watched his display, her mouth open slightly.

With a derisive shake of his head, Parker turned back toward his truck. Joe and Bud were already in the truck, Bud in the passenger seat, and Joe in the back seat of the extended cab. Parker did one last quick scan of the construction site and, satisfied that everything had been gathered up, climbed up behind the wheel.

"I don't know about you guys," he said, "but I could sure use a cold beer or three."

Kenzie Stewart looked up at the clock on the wall. Three o'clock. Two more hours and she would be going home. She remembered a time when that would have been a relief. Lately, though, she had noticed almost a feeling of dread.

Not that her job offered a great deal of satisfaction. She didn't feel like she was taken seriously. Her thoughts and ideas were routinely shot down in favor of those of other employees with more seniority, or higher degrees. Or a penis.

At least that's the way it felt.

Kenzie sat back in her chair and tilted her head back, allowing her long, luxuriant red hair to hang down behind her. She took a deep breath and remembered a time when she was happy. Even now, she *seemed* happy to everyone who met her. She just had a naturally bubbly personality. But it didn't seem to reach into her real life anymore. She felt almost like two different people.

In an effort to shake off her dark mood, she decided to take a stroll through the displays. She stood up and took another deep breath, rotating her head, stretching her neck in an effort to relax.

She felt Brad watching her, but she tried to ignore it. Brad Mitchell was the manager, the one who most often disregarded her suggestions. She wasn't sure if it was because he didn't take her seriously, or because she had rebuffed his advances a few months before. She sometimes got mixed messages from him.

She left the office at the back of the gallery and walked slowly into the main area. A couple of people were wandering aimlessly through the space, but Kenzie could tell at a glance they were not seriously considering a purchase. She had learned to read the signals that people gave off. She directed her attention, instead, to the art, and as was usually the case, she felt herself start to relax.

Gallery BC was tucked between a trendy brew pub and a trendy gift shop in equally trendy Larimer Square, a one block shopping and dining area on the oldest street in downtown Denver, Colorado. The "BC" in the gallery's name stood for Betty and Carl Morgan, the couple who had started the gallery twenty years before. The gallery had been a venture they started in their fifties. Now in their seventies, they were not so active in the business any longer.

They left that to their small staff.

The first space Kenzie came to was a display of photography and multimedia pieces from a local photographer and her boyfriend. Kenzie had known JuleighAnn Harper for a few years, ever since Bobby, Kenzie's brother, had died from a malignant brain tumor. JuleighAnn worked as a counselor and had helped her family through that ordeal. She and Kenzie had remained friends ever since.

As Facebook friends, Kenzie had seen some of the photographs that JuleighAnn regularly posted on her page, and had always thought that her work deserved to be seen by more than just a few online friends. When JuleighAnn's boyfriend, Arden Chase, arranged a small exhibit in the lobby of a downtown hotel a few months back, Kenzie approached her about an extended exhibit at the gallery.

She had feared the Morgans would think she wanted to sign JuleighAnn based solely on her friendship with her. But they were immediately taken with JuleighAnn's somber and moody photographs of the parks, woods and wildlife surrounding the lake where she lived, and indeed, the JuleighAnn Harper exhibit proved to be one of their most popular ones.

That was the last of Kenzie's suggestions that had actually been taken seriously.

She felt her phone vibrate and she fished it out of her pocket. Seeing the display, the relaxation she had just cultivated vaporized instantly. She pushed her abundant red hair out of the way and put the phone to her ear.

"Hi Jim," she answered.

"Hey babe," her husband replied. Jim's work hours got him home well before Kenzie. "You got something in the mail from somebody named Anthony Pine. Looks like a greeting card. Who's Anthony Pine?"

"I'm sorry, I don't know anybody named Anthony Pine," Kenzie said, feeling her heart quicken a bit.

"Why would a total stranger be sending you a card?"

"Honey, I honestly don't know an Anthony Pine. I'm sorry, but I don't know what it could be."

"You're telling me a complete stranger is sending shit addressed personally to you?"

"I guess so, Jim," Kenzie replied, trying not to sound impatient with him.

"Do you want me to open it?" Jim asked. Kenzie always thought that was a dumb question. Every time he asked it. Why would she *want* him to open her mail? A more accurate question would be, 'Do *I* want to open your mail?'

Kenzie knew the answer to that one.

"That's fine, Jim, go ahead." She waited while she heard paper tearing in the background. There was a pause, and Jim came back on.

"Oh, it's just one of those car sale notices." She had been seeing a few of those lately, direct mail ads made to look like a personal greeting card, addressed by hand. "False alarm. I'll let you get back to work."

"Okay, Jim," Kenzie said, struggling to keep the irritation out of her voice.

"Maybe I'll take you out to dinner tonight," he said. "Feel like a steak? We could go to Outback."

"Sure, that sounds good. I should be home at my usual time."

"Okay, babe. See you then."

Kenzie put the phone in her pocket and directed her attention back to the photographs on the wall. Her calm was shattered. Now the pictures didn't look as peaceful as they did before. Instead, they just seemed brooding.

Perfect. They matched her mood.

Hunter Sage watched impassively as the forest blurred past on both sides as he drove west on Durham Road, Highway 98 out of Raleigh, North Carolina. For a moment, he imagined the dramatic and fiery scene that might result if he quickly turned his wheel and plowed his Chevy Impala into the trees.

Hunter's steely-grey eyes surveyed the passing forest, taking note that several of the tree trunks were plenty big enough to do the job. His gas tank was almost full. With enough speed, if he made it count . . . .

With a sigh and a force of will, Hunter focused his attention back on the road in front of him and absently rubbed his left wrist. The raised scars often itched when he was disturbed or irritated, as he was now. He scratched the scar on his left wrist and switched to the right one as he passed a slow-moving pickup.

He was receiving faulty messages from his brain. That's the way Dr. Jeffries explained it anyway. Grief was natural. The desire to do himself harm was not.

Like his brother, Parker, Hunter was good looking and well-built, though not as muscular. His looks might be categorized as ruggedly handsome. He was also dark. Dark hair, dark grey eyes, and a dark countenance born of having seen too much.

If someone said that Hunter and Parker were brothers, and they were seen standing side by side, one might be able to pick out enough similarities to support that theory. But they were different enough that it had been a long-standing family joke that Parker, the younger brother, looked like the mailman.

As Hunter continued his drive, his surroundings gradually became more industrial as a sign welcomed him to Allure, and he heaved a sigh that would have been audible if anyone had been with him.

Allure, North Carolina languished between Raleigh and Durham without contributing much to either, an industrial pothole on the road connecting two destinations. Despite its name, and its location in the picturesque forested hills, Allure was anything but alluring. It was a grim, dirty little town, often used as a pit stop for drug dealers and other undesirables.

In the past couple of decades, several businesses had relocated to the larger cities, leaving behind empty hulks of buildings unsuitable for other uses without massive renovations. The cost of such renovations was prohibitive to the smaller industries still located there, so much of Allure remained an industrial ghost town.

Attempts to clean up the town and its reputation had ultimately met with disappointment. People passing through tended to hurry by, to get to whichever place they actually wanted to go to, so that they had to spend no more time in Allure than was necessary to get from point A to point B.

Hunter didn't have that luxury. He pulled into his driveway and shut off the engine. Gathering up the file folder from the passenger seat, he got out of his car and dragged his feet up to the front door of his house. The folder had papers peeking out the edge and he purposely pushed them back in without looking at them.

Entering the house, the dust and the clutter registered, but just barely, and he continued through the living room. At the sound of his entry, Jarvis slunk into view but displayed indifference.

Jarvis was Katherine's orange tabby and had never demonstrated much interest in Hunter. To be fair, Hunter had never really cared for cats either.

"I guess the cleaning lady didn't come today," Hunter said to the cat. Jarvis blankly looked up at Hunter, then weaved around his leg, getting as much cat hair on his pants as he could. "You know, you could help out a little around here."

In an often repeated routine, Hunter deposited his keys on the side table near the door to the kitchen, followed by his gun. This used to be followed by his badge, but as a private detective, he didn't have to carry an actual badge any longer. The folder was a new twist on the routine, but still he ignored it, placing it next to the other items, still unopened.

He continued into the kitchen where he dropped a couple of ice cubes in a glass and dribbled some Jim Beam over them. Hunter took a sip and sighed. He eased down onto a stool at the counter and looked at the picture of Katherine that he kept there. Jarvis jumped up onto the counter in front of him and Hunter brushed him off.

"How many times do I gotta tell you? Stay off the counters!" Jarvis seemed insulted by the affront, or maybe it was just Hunter's imagination. At any rate, the cat skulked away, presumably going to one of the many locations in the house where he liked to hide.

"What the hell am I going to do, Kath?" Hunter sighed, looking at her picture. She silently stared back at him with her frozen smile and her happy green eyes, her auburn hair cascading over her shoulders. "It's been nearly three years and I'm still not over it." Hunter continued looking at Katherine, but there was no answer, and he wearily rubbed his face, then drained the last of his bourbon.

He reached for the bottle and poured a little more into the glass. Carrying it with him, he got up and went back to the living room, and he looked down at the folder on the table. As if steeling himself for the effort, he drew a deep breath and picked up the folder. He clutched it tightly, slowly exhaling the breath as he walked, and carried it to the worn right side of the love seat where he sat down in his usual spot.

He was careful to leave Katherine's side untouched, as always.

He opened the folder and began shuffling through the papers and photographs.

Victim: Katherine Sage.

Hunter put the photographs aside, face down, and without looking at them. He knew he wasn't ready for that yet. He wasn't entirely sure he was ready for the rest of it either. Neither was Dr. Jeffries.

"That could be disastrous," Dr. Jeffries had said yesterday morning. "Reopening wounds you've been trying to heal. Investigating her case could just freshen and revitalize your grief."

Hunter still saw the psychiatrist on a weekly basis, every Thursday. Even though he was no longer on the force and the visits were not mandatory, he knew they helped.

"I understand, Doc," Hunter replied. "But I feel like I've got to do this. I think that part of what's making it hard to heal is that it's unsolved. You yourself are the one who talked about closure. I feel like this is what I need to do to have closure." Dr. Jeffries studied Hunter's face for a moment.

"I guess you *have* been listening to what I've said," he finally responded with a slight smile. "Though I'm not really sure about the application."

"Well, I can't say I'm sure either, but I need to give it a try."

"My main concern is your history."

"I know," Hunter nodded. "I don't blame you. I'm concerned too. But I haven't been suicidal at all in the past year."

18

"Well," Dr. Jeffries countered, drawing out the word with a disbelieving tone in his voice, "you've said the thoughts have been there. You may not have tried to act on them again, but with the thoughts there beneath the surface, don't you think that the stress and emotion of looking into Katherine's case could be a catalyst?"

"I don't know," Hunter replied, shaking his head. He rubbed the scars on his wrists. "But I feel like I need to do something, and not just for myself. I feel like I owe it to Katherine to try to solve her murder."

Dr. Jeffries had continued questioning him for a few minutes after that, but Hunter decided it was just to test his resolve and his emotional competence. In the end, he had finally acquiesced and promised to make a call to Captain Oates.

Today, Hunter had been able to pick up a copy of Katherine's file. It felt strange being back in the police station, seeing the old, familiar faces looking at him, now with pity. He didn't stay to visit with anyone. He picked up the folder from Oates and left the station, his errand done in less than five minutes.

The problem was that he didn't find anything in the report that he didn't already know. The only description they had of the killer was male, average height, average build, no face.

After perusing it for a half hour, he closed the file, shook his head and picked up his bourbon.

ily Sage walked through the house dusting. She took it slowly, knowing how fatigued she could get. She brushed her Swiffer duster across the top of the dining room chairs, and then on the table. She leaned on the edge of it to support herself as she reached across the table. She felt it give way a little and she remembered, taking her weight off of it.

Parker had been saying he was going to fix the table, but hadn't gotten around to it yet. A support or something, under the table, had come loose. It wasn't a priority, though, because they seldom ate in the dining room. So it regularly got moved to the bottom of his to do list. She brushed a tear away, not knowing why it had come, not even thinking about it anymore.

Even though it was late afternoon, little light penetrated the blinds and curtains. Lily preferred it dark. She knew that Parker would have a problem with it, so she planned to open them before he got home. But she also knew that he was going to the bar with his crew after work, so she still had some time.

The light just felt so harsh, so unforgiving. The dark, on the other hand, was relaxing and welcoming. Lily felt as if she could breathe more easily in the dim light.

It was all in her head. She knew that. Many sessions with Jane, her therapist, had convinced her of that. But that didn't make it feel any less real. If she went outside, which she didn't if she could avoid it, the severe, burning sunlight pressed down on her with a physical weight. She could feel that weight lift off of her when she came back inside.

It hadn't always been that way.

Back when Lily and Kathy were in high school, they practically lived on the beach. At that time, they lived in Washington, North Carolina, a little town east of Greenville, on the Pamlico River. There were times when certain favorite spots along the river served as their beach, but during the warmer months, they spent almost every weekend on the Outer Banks. Lily's father had owned a small cottage near the beach, and in the summer, that became their home away from home.

Lily and Katherine were inseparable. If somebody saw Kathy's fiery auburn hair, they knew that Lily's blazing golden hair would be nearby.

Even after their schooling was finished, they remained best friends. Their lives were inextricably linked, even to the point of falling in love with and marrying brothers. Lily remembered loving the fact that she and her best friend had the same last name.

Parker had been absolutely taken with Lily. And such a romantic! Their first year together, Lily would find a fresh bouquet of roses in a vase on the dining room table every Monday morning, until she told him to stop or they would go broke.

Lily had been so pretty back then. And God, what a hunk of beefcake Parker was! Sandy colored hair, with sparkling blue eyes and an adorable dimple on each side of his smile. And that muscular body! Not so much like Arnold Schwarzenegger. More like Matthew McConaughey at his best.

Lily hadn't realized that she liked tattoos until she saw them on Parker. Beautiful, intricate designs, weaving their way across his back and shoulders, and down his left arm. She remembered following the pattern with her fingers, tracing a particular path across his back, around his shoulder and ending up at his nipple. She quickly remembered which lines led there, to tease him, which usually resulted in him returning the favor with her own nipples.

Sex almost always ensued, and it was always good. Parker was a tender, attentive lover, always concerned with her satisfaction so that, even if she didn't cum, which was rare, it was still a wonderfully pleasurable experience. He had managed to find erogenous zones she didn't know she had, spots on or in her body that produced the most incredible, toe-curling sensations.

Parker's brother, Hunter, from what Kathy had told her, was similarly attentive. Kathy had said she had never felt so loved. Hunter, while different from Parker, was still well-built, and he was handsome, but with an edge. Lily wondered if that edge came from being a cop.

But he loved Kathy and lived for her happiness!

Everything changed on Labor Day, almost three years ago. Lily had tortured herself ever since then with 'what ifs.'

What if she and Kathy had lingered just a little longer over lunch? She had heard of the "butterfly effect." Minor differences in action could have major effects on the outcome. If they had relaxed and lingered at the restaurant, they would have gotten to the shopping center later, and parked in a different location.

What if she had given in when Kathy wanted to go to Panera Bread for lunch, instead of insisting they go to Chili's? Then they wouldn't have even been in that part of town.

What if Kathy and Hunter hadn't argued that morning? Then Kathy probably wouldn't have sent a message to Lily, wanting to get out and vent.

It was all useless. Events in the past were locked immutably in the past, no matter how hard Lily wished things had been done differently.

Kathy and Hunter *had* argued that morning. Lily *did* insist that she wanted to go to Chili's. And she *had* been anxious to get out of the restaurant and enjoy the sunny day.

And now, Kathy was dead.

Lily's hair was darker now, since she seldom went outside. Conversely, her skin was lighter, but for the same reason. Parker was still attentive to her needs, but sex had become fairly rare. He accepted her depression, even understood it, and he never complained about their diminished sex life.

Which seemed to make her feel even worse.

She felt guilty about being unable to make love to Parker very often. She felt guilty about actions and decisions in the past that led to Kathy's death. And she felt guilty about the cost of the medications and the sessions with Jane, expenses she knew they couldn't afford.

She knew she couldn't help it, but she still felt guilty.

The Sawmill was a rowdy place, north of Raleigh, and right on the highway. Pickups and motorcycles filled the parking lot. It was the kind of bar that usually had country music blaring from the jukebox, and everybody had to shout to be heard over it, and over the others vying to be heard. The two pool tables in the back were usually in use, sometimes with short stacks of money on the rails.

Parker and his crew stopped in there a couple times a week after work. Bud, the extrovert, fit in very well with the rowdy crowd, while Parker and Joe were usually quieter. Bud was barely in the door when he started loudly calling out to friends he saw and performing various forms of handshakes. Parker and Joe smiled and greeted friends as they passed, and only occasionally shook hands.

Thad, the bartender, saw them coming and had three cold beers waiting for them by the time they arrived at the bar. They approached the end of the bar nearest the door, where the music was not quite so loud.

"Good to see you, Thad," Parker said with a nod. Thad nodded back and smiled, but turned immediately to fill another order. The three men clinked their glasses together and drank. Their glasses were half empty when they put them down. They had just turned around and leaned back against the bar when they saw an attractive woman who looked to be in her fifties, dressed in a black business-like pant suit, making her way through the press of bodies. She was approaching the trio with focused determination. Her focus was on Parker.

Parker watched with a measure of apprehension. He wasn't sure what to make of this woman twenty years his senior, as she pushed through the crowd toward him, her eyes sliding up and down his body with slippery abandon. As her eyes lingered in one spot in particular, he wondered if he had left his fly open.

She stopped less than two feet away, her red open-toed Ferragamos nearly touching his work boots. From close up, she looked Parker up and down one more time, then she looked him hard in the eyes.

"Damn, son," she finally said, "what's your name?"

"Parker, ma'am," he replied suspiciously. "And yours?"

"Marlys," she said, her voice so dripping with lust, Parker had the urge to check and see if she had gotten any on the top of his boots. "Marlys Rosenfeldt."

Parker cleared his throat nervously.

"Something I can do for you, Ms. Rosenfeldt?"

"As a matter of fact, there is," the woman said, and Parker felt Bud's elbow in his ribs. He tried to ignore it and focus his attention on what Marlys was saying. "My friends and I are putting together a little project that I think you would be perfect for."

Only at this point did they see the young man and woman who were apparently with her, finally squeezing through the crowd and coming up behind her. It was also at this time that Parker realized he may have misread the message that Marlys had been sending him.

"You've probably seen those calendars with a photo of a hunky man for each month," Marlys continued. "We're creating one focusing on working men of North Carolina, and we've had a last minute dropout. I was really pissed 'cause it put a ginormous crimp in our schedule. But now, I'm glad it happened. I think you'd make a perfect Mr. October, Parker."

Parker glanced nervously at his two friends, then back at the woman.

"I don't know, Ms. Rosenfeldt. That doesn't really sound like me."

"We'll pay you five hundred dollars on the spot," she continued undeterred, "and it will only take an hour or two of your time."

"Five hundred dollars?" Parker echoed. Lily's mounting therapy and prescription bills came to mind. "I could use that."

"Perhaps we could step outside where it's a little quieter. We just have a very short, simple contract and a release form for you to sign."

Kenzie Stewart collapsed on the sofa as Jim headed upstairs to bed. Dinner at Outback Steakhouse had been good, as always. It was the time with Jim that Kenzie found increasingly difficult. She thought back on the evening, trying to determine if there was anything she did that had brought it on. Anything she could have done differently.

It was nearly six o'clock when she arrived at their home in Englewood, in the Denver Tech Center, southeast of Denver, and Jim was already impatient.

"It usually takes you thirty to forty-five minutes to get home," he said accusingly. "What took you so long?"

"There was an accident on I-25," she replied. "I was just past the Belleview exit when I hit the backup. It took me over twenty minutes just to get to the next exit at Orchard."

"You could have called," Jim said. "You knew I was waiting. You knew we had plans."

"I'm sorry. My phone battery was low and I wanted to save it in case of emergency."

He had looked at her for a moment as if he were trying to decide whether or not to believe her story. After a few seconds, he sighed and shook his head, his eyebrows raised.

"Okay, fine. Well, let's get going," he said impatiently, as if Kenzie's answering his question was now the reason they were late.

When they finally arrived at the restaurant, they had to wait for a table, and Jim was angry about that too.

"If we'd gotten here fifteen minutes ago, they probably could have seated us right away!" he said. He held Kenzie's gaze with a piercing stare for a few moments afterward to drive home the point that it was because of her they had to wait.

After they had been seated, during the time after they ordered but before the food arrived, Kenzie had to listen to details of his day. A few years ago, that hadn't been a problem. In fact, they both had listened to the details of each other's day. But now, it was pretty much just Jim complaining about his job. A pressman for a print shop, he had issues with his press, or with a customer, or with a coworker, or with his employer. There was always something wrong.

When his steak arrived, and it was a little too done for his taste, he complained to the waitress about it. He didn't send it back, but he wanted it made very clear that he wasn't happy. The whole time, Kenzie kept her head inclined a bit, her thick red hair pulled over her shoulder like a curtain, shielding her from the eyes of those around them who could surely hear Jim's tirade. Instead, she kept her eyes focused on her own plate, embarrassed for the waitress, not wanting to peek around the curtain for fear her intuition was correct, that people were looking at them, talking about them.

Then they came home. And she heard another familiar complaint.

"Why don't you ever come to bed with me?" he asked. "You always make me go to bed alone."

"Jim, you get up three hours earlier than I do," Kenzie protested. Again. "I'm sorry, but I can't just fall asleep at eight o'clock."

"Well it's too bad you can't find it in your heart to adjust your fucking schedule so you can actually go to bed with your husband." He was tired, so beyond that statement, there was no extended argument about it this time. But again, he sternly held her gaze.

"I'm tired," he finally said with a sigh and an exasperated shake of his head. "I'm going to bed." And he went upstairs.

Yes, being a difficult, unhappy douche bag must be *extremely* tiring.

Kenzie felt bad, as she usually did, about his final accusation, that she never went to bed the same time as he did. But she couldn't think of anything she could have done to make the evening before that turn out any differently. She felt the tears coming but she fought them back. She needed a distraction.

She pushed herself up from the sofa and got her phone out of her purse. She hadn't had a chance to charge it yet, but she kept a USB charger plugged in beside the sofa. She attached the USB plug to her phone and woke it up, and she touched the Facebook icon.

Parker got up from the bed when he was certain Lily was asleep. It had become his habit to sit with her until whatever anxiety or fear was affecting her at the time had passed and her breathing became slower and steady, indicating the beginning of her sleep pattern. As he left the bedroom, he thought, as he often did, about taking one of her Trimipramine capsules. He never did follow through on it, but God! It had become such a chore to be around Lily. At times, he felt like he needed an anti-depressant just to be with her.

Parker dragged himself into the living room and collapsed on the sofa. He put his head back, closed his eyes, and sighed, sitting perfectly still for a few seconds. Finally, he sat up, pulled out his phone and punched a number on his "favorites" menu.

"Hello?" said a familiar voice on the other end.

"Hey, Hunter," Parker said. "It's me."

"Hey, little brother. What's up?"

Parker sighed again, trying to assemble his thoughts.

"I don't know, man. I just feel like I've almost had enough."

"Lily, you mean?"

"Yeah. And I feel like such a shit, too, because I know she can't help it. But she's just making me crazy."

"Something happen tonight?"

"Oh, not really anything in particular. Nothing out of the ordinary, I mean. Just the tears and the stares off into the distance. She'll just be sitting there perfectly still with a blank look on her face, and then suddenly jump, like somebody sprang up in front of her."

"Maybe her medications need to be adjusted," Hunter suggested.

"Yeah, maybe. They just adjusted them a couple of weeks ago. I mean they've got her on an antidepressant medication and an anti-anxiety medication, and some others that I'm not entirely sure what they're for. I'm going broke from all these drugs and her therapy sessions."

"Do you love her?"

Parker paused, startled by the question. He raised his free hand up to his face and rubbed his eyes. He took a deep breath and held it while he thought. He let it out as he replied.

"I'm not sure any more. And that's why I feel like such a shit. Like I said, I know she can't help the way she's become."

"Don't beat yourself up about it, Parker. Not everybody's cut out to be a caretaker. It's hard work."

"I know, but she's my wife. There was that 'in sickness and in health' thing in our vows."

"That's right," Hunter replied, "but you know what? You need to take care of yourself, too. You know those pre-flight instructions flight attendants give that nobody ever listens to? You know how they say that if the cabin loses pressure, the oxygen masks will drop down, and you're supposed to put your own on before helping anybody else with theirs?"

"Yeah, I've heard that."

"They don't say that to give you permission to be selfish. Fact is, if you pass out from lack of oxygen, you won't be any good to anybody else. It's important for you to take care of your own needs."

"You're telling me to leave her?"

"No, I'm not. I can't tell you that. I'm saying that *you* need to decide what's best for you."

Parker thought for a moment.

"Well," he said slowly, as if trying out the words, "she doesn't have any siblings, but her parents are only in their fifties. And they've got a little money. So I guess if I *did* leave her, it's not like she would just be abandoned. They'd take care of her. Probably better than I could, in fact."

Hunter was silent.

"What do you think?" Parker asked.

"I think you need to make your own decision, little brother. That's not something somebody else can decide for you."

"God, I'd look like such a shit to our friends and neighbors."

"Parker, you need to stop thinking about how you look to other people and start thinking about what you're able to handle yourself."

"I know," Parker said with a sigh. "You're right."

"Of course, I am," Hunter replied. "I'm the smarter brother, remember? Now get some rest, okay?"

"Yeah. Thanks, man."

Parker broke the connection and sat there, lost in thought. The idea had never occurred to him that he could leave Lily. What he had told Hunter was true: He wasn't sure if he even loved her any longer. She was so different from the beautiful, happy girl he married. She was still pretty – or she could be. But she was so far from happy. He couldn't remember the last time she smiled. And any time he spent with her just brought him down, too.

He looked down at the phone still in his hand. He touched the Facebook icon and watched as the app started up. He was struck by the first thing he saw:

> Those who are unhappy have no need for anything in this world but people capable of giving them their attention.
> - Simone Weil

Posted by a pretty redhead in Colorado, Kenzie Stewart, that line struck a note that resonated with Parker. He clicked on Kenzie's name and saw they weren't Facebook friends. Confused, he went back to his news feed. Then he saw that a mutual friend had commented on Kenzie's status, simply typing ":(" which Facebook translated into a little yellow frowning face. That mutual friend's sympathy was the reason why it showed up on Parker's news feed.

Parker reread the line, he clicked on Kenzie's name, then the "Add Friend" button.

Kenzie was just about to close her Facebook app when she got a notice of a friend request. Parker Sage, a man in North Carolina, had made contact. Curious about how he found her, she looked at his profile page. They had a mutual Facebook friend, who had just commented on her recent status update.

But she was quickly distracted from that when she saw his pictures. Good God! The man looked like he just stepped off the cover of a romance novel. Impossibly handsome, with more muscles than one man would ever use. Crystal blue eyes, dimpled cheeks, gorgeous smile. The man was a poster child for Heartbreakers of America!

She pulled herself away from his photos page to his personal information.

"Dammit!" she thought. "He's married." Then she scoffed to herself. "What am I thinking? I'm married too."

She backed up to the page that contained his friend request, and she accepted it. Almost immediately, she received a personal message in Facebook Messenger from her gorgeous new friend.

"Hi. Thanks for the friendship."

"Thanks for the request," Kenzie responded.

"What kind of name is Kenzie?"

"It's short for Mackenzie. It's Scottish. It means 'fair one'."

"It's a pretty name. So, you're in Denver. I've always wanted to visit Colorado, but never have yet."

"Colorado's nice, but I live and work in the city. Probably much like any other city."

"Yeah, I reckon parts of Raleigh could maybe pass for any city too."

"I reckon?" Kenzie replied. "You're a southern boy with a southern drawl, aren't you?"

"Well, yes ma'am, Ah s'pose Ah do talk with a li'l bit o' that there southern accent."

Kenzie snorted.

"Now you're just making fun of me."

"No, I wouldn't do that. I'm also a southern gentleman. I would never make fun of a lady."

"How do you know I'm a lady?"

"Well now, since we just met, that's a good point. So tell me about yourself."

"There's not much to tell, really," she typed. "I'm thirty-one years old and I work in an art gallery in downtown Denver."

"And you're married."

"Yes, I am. My husband, Jim, is a pressman in a print shop."

Was it her imagination, or did she really tense up when she typed that one sentence about Jim? She suddenly wanted to change the subject, and she glanced at Parker's picture again. Interestingly, the tension remained, but it was a different kind, felt a little lower.

"So what about you, Parker?" she continued. "Are you a bodybuilder?"

"No. People always ask me that. I'm a building contractor. I build houses."

Kenzie paused, wanting to continue talking about his build, but not knowing if she should. Parker apparently noticed the pause and started typing again.

"Must just be the job and good genes, I guess."

I guess! Kenzie said under her breath.

"So," Parker continued, on a different tack, "you like southern boys?"

"Excuse me?" Kenzie typed, taken a little by surprise.

"You asked if I was a southern boy with a southern drawl. Just wondering if you like the south or not."

Uh oh. Time for some diplomacy.

"You know, to be perfectly frank, I've never really been drawn to the south, but honestly, I haven't really had much exposure to it either."

"But you kinda like the accent though, right?"

Shit!

"Okay, I'll be honest with you," she typed, taking her time to try to offend as little as possible. "I've heard a lot about southern hospitality and the charm of the south, but the fact is I've always been a little turned off by the accent."

"Turned off?! Ma'am, I think we might be gon' have us a smidge of trouble here."

Kenzie sighed and shook her head, but with a bit of a smile at Parker's humor.

"I'm sorry," she replied, "but it's always just sounded kind of 'back woods' and uneducated to me. You know, the Honey Boo Boo and Duck Dynasty crowd just never appealed to me. But it's just as likely it was only those kinds of southerners that I've been exposed to."

"Yeah, I have to admit they haven't done much for our image."

"Maybe southern gentlemen are different."

As she reread the messages she had just sent, she cringed at how Parker must be taking that. Hoping to stem his offense, she started typing again.

"I'm just getting myself in deeper and deeper, aren't I? I'm sorry, Parker. As I read that, I realized that this is probably just an unfounded personal prejudice I need to get over."

Parker responded simply with a smiley. Kenzie sighed.

"In fact," she continued, "I'm sure that's it, because YOU seem to express yourself very well. So I'm just going to shut up now and work on prying my foot from my mouth."

"No, don't worry about it," Parker replied. "You're fine. I don't suppose the south can be everybody's cup of tea. Don't want it to get too crowded down here, anyway." He followed it with another smiley.

"So, I noticed you're married, too," Kenzie said, relieved to change the subject.

"Yes, I am," he replied. "Lily. We been married for about seven years."

"Yeah? What does Lily do?"

There was a noticeable pause before Parker started typing again.

"Not a whole hell of a lot," he said. "Listen, I won't suck you into my problems. Let's just say my life is a little bit less than ideal."

"I'm sorry. I didn't mean to pry."

"You weren't. You were just making conversation. Nothing wrong with that. But listen, I should let you go. I need to get up early tomorrow."

"Okay, Parker. Very nice meeting you."

"You too."

And he was gone. Kenzie read through their conversation for a moment, shrinking a little into the sofa as she read her comments about the south and southern accents. No wonder he left in such a hurry! But as she continued looking at their exchange, she realized that he seemed to be okay with those remarks. It was only after Kenzie asked about his wife that Parker felt compelled to cut off the conversation.

I wonder what's up with Lily, she thought as she closed Facebook.

This is perfect," Marlys said as she looked around the construction site. She turned to Jem, the young African American man at her side. There was a camera hanging around his neck. "You can shoot in that direction," she said as she pointed toward the back of the site. "You'll have all those skeletal walls behind him, but no other houses to distract from it. Just the woods."

"Looks good," Jem replied as he looked around, his shoulder-length braids dangling around his face. "I was thinking we'd have to wait until the sun was higher, but it's looking good now. Good, sharp contrast."

"Great!" Marlys looked at Jem. "I appreciate you making time for this on such short notice."

"Not a problem. I had a cancellation myself. If your original October hadn't cancelled, I would have just spent the weekend drinking too much."

"Yeah?" Marlys smiled at him. "Well, let's see if our boy's ready."

She carefully stepped down off the subflooring and foundation, and walked toward the blue portable toilet, smiling at the company's name, Scotty's Pottys. Parker had gone in there five minutes ago. Surely he must be changed by now.

"Parker," she called, "how's it going?"

"Uh, fine, ma'am," came a timid reply. "Sorry, I don't mean to be piddling around, but are you sure about this?"

"Sure about what, hon?"

The fastener on the door rattled and the plastic door swung outward. Parker stood there, wearing an embarrassed expression and not much else. The denim cutoffs would have been a little small on Daisy Duke. He looked down at the straining zipper, and at the button which wouldn't even reach the buttonhole, leaving the waistband open. And the waistband was cut so low, the top of his pubic hair was even showing.

"There's gotta be a mistake," he said. "Somebody got the wrong size."

Marlys looked appreciatively at the diminutive shorts. Parker had carefully positioned his genitals to the side, so they were still covered by the small shorts. But the tightness of the shorts just made them stand out even more, and their corresponding bulges seemed to be enhanced by the positioning. And recalling an old Robin Williams joke, Marlys could even tell what religion he was.

"No, there's no mistake," Marlys said with a libidinous smile. She took his arm and guided him out. Then she stepped back, to take in the whole picture. His physique was gorgeous. The tight muscles, covered with the smooth, golden-brown skin, made her heart flutter a little. The tattoos were a nice touch. Not overdone, but expertly tracing the contours of his body, and twining around his left nipple. She loved that.

She paused again at the shorts, feeling herself getting a little damp down below, then let her eyes slide down his sturdy brown legs to his work boots, and finally, slowly, back up to his face. His piercing blue eyes were watching her.

"You look great, hon," Marlys said. "Really! I think you're gonna be the highlight of the calendar." Parker seemed to relax a bit at that, and even smiled a little, causing the dimples to make an appearance. Marlys nodded. "Yeah, and you have to smile for the pictures," she said. "The ladies are gonna absolutely fall in love with those dimples!"

"Okay," he responded, barely above a whisper. He still didn't seem sure about it, but at least he was going along with it.

"Come on, son, let's get started. Jem said the light's just perfect right now." She put her arm through his as she guided him back toward the structure, and she smiled as she felt his arm flex a little at her touch. Spurred on by the flex, she purposefully wrapped her fingers around the solid bicep and leaned against him as they walked, hoping the panty liner she was wearing would be enough to contain what she felt down there. "I'm glad you recommended shooting here," she continued, forcing her voice to be steady. "I think this will be a perfect backdrop for your pictures."

"Well, ma'am, I knew nobody would be here on a Saturday morning. And it's where I'm working now, so it just kinda made sense. Just be careful, though. I know our insurance wouldn't cover injuries sustained during a modeling gig." His voice sounded a little strained, but he smiled at his attempt at humor. Marlys smiled in return, and squeezed his bicep as Parker helped her up onto the plywood subflooring.

Jem watched as they approached. He watched Parker for a moment, then looked at Marlys with a smile and one eyebrow raised. Marlys knew very little about Jem's personal life. He never spoke about his sexual orientation or preference. During photo shoots, he verbally made love to the models, appreciating and optimizing the qualities of beauty of either gender, and Marlys suspected he might be bisexual.

On the other hand, maybe that was just the mark of a good photographer. Either way, Marlys knew he approved.

She picked up Parker's tool belt from the floor and handed it to him.

"Are you sure this won't cover up too much?" Parker asked, raising one eyebrow. Marlys could hear the sarcasm in his voice, and she smiled again.

"I'm thinking it will cover just enough of the shorts to make it look like there's even less."

Parker buckled the belt in place, and he saw what she meant. The top of the belt came just above the waistband of the cutoffs, and only a bit of denim showed between the pouches. But somehow, feeling the belt, feeling the handle of his hammer against his leg, made him a little more comfortable.

"Okay, babe," Jem said, motioning toward the framed wall behind Parker, "right over there. We'll start with some simple shots of you standing in front of your construction, and then we'll see where that leads us."

Marlys watched appreciatively as Jem directed Parker into different poses, snapping pictures along the way. Despite the early hour, it was already getting warm as she felt the sun beating down on her back and shoulder. She slipped off the jacket of her pant suit and draped it over her arm as she watched quietly behind Jem.

She was happy to see Parker was feeling the heat too, as his skin began glistening in the early morning sunlight, creating a rippling sheen that she found particularly attractive. He still seemed a little nervous, but he was trying to get into the spirit.

Marlys thought at first that he was nervous about posing in such a state of undress. But she remembered how readily he opened the door of the portable toilet when she was there, and she realized he was probably just uncomfortable about striking suggestive poses in front of another man.

Marlys looked around for ideas to help him relax, and in so doing, noticed a young lady, a pretty blonde, standing at the window of the house just to the south, only partly concealed by the shadows of the interior. She was intently watching the proceedings, and didn't even notice Marlys looking at her.

Marlys smiled and turned, walking a few steps toward Parker.

"Looks like you have a rapt audience," she whispered with a slight tilt of her head. Parker looked up, following the direction of Marlys' head tilt, and saw the pretty blonde looking at him. "Make love to her," Marlys said.

Parker looked at Marlys for a moment, alarmed, until he got her meaning. He looked back toward the window, smiled at the young woman, and began flexing his muscles, striking suggestive poses in her direction. Marlys glanced at the window again. The young lady had stepped closer, now almost fully visible, her breasts rising and falling with her breathing.

The window sill was at about the level of her waist. Marlys could see her left hand clenched tightly on the window sill.

She couldn't see where her right hand was, but she had a suspicion.

Kenzie woke up slowly, feeling the morning wrap itself around her. She stretched luxuriously and turned her head, seeing exactly what she expected to see. The other side of the bed was empty. Jim had likely been up for at least a couple of hours.

Turning the other direction, she looked at her clock. It was nearly eight o'clock. About as late as she ever slept on the weekend. She knew that Jim would be with Rick by now. He and a friend he worked with were building a Model T, and they always got together on Saturday mornings at his house, because Rick had a large garage where they were able to work.

As she got out of bed, Kenzie knew she had at least four hours to herself.

Within minutes, she had coffee brewing, and as she waited, she looked out the kitchen window. It faced west, toward the mountains, but she could only see a tiny sliver of them. Beyond the houses in her neighborhood, the skyline of the Denver Technological Center, a business district south of Denver, stood between her and the mountains.

She sighed. She worked among the tall buildings of downtown Denver all week. She was a city girl, born and raised in Denver, so she liked it, but she liked the mountains, too. She loved being able to see nature. But on the weekend, when she didn't have to be downtown, all the houses, and the buildings of DTC blocked her view of the mountains.

She looked again at the note that Jim had left.

Breakfast alone again. I missed you.

She knew this message was something else she would have to keep to herself. She knew from experience that others would likely misconstrue it. People she had told in the past about Jim's notes and comments thought he sounded like a dreamy romantic. 'He missed you. He wants to have breakfast with you. How sweet!'

In the context of their *real* relationship, Kenzie knew this note was simply another of Jim's passive-aggressive criticisms of her, similar to his complaining last night about her never going to bed with him.

She wadded up the note and tossed it in the trash. She reached into the cabinet and got a coffee cup, noticing that her hand was shaking a little, and she poured a cup of coffee. She held the cup to her lips with both hands as she thought about the one person she could talk to freely about Jim. JuleighAnn Harper, the photographer, the grief counselor turned friend, had been sympathetic since the first time Kenzie had revealed Jim's subtle darker undercurrent. Kenzie realized that she hadn't seen JuleighAnn in a couple of weeks, since the opening of her exhibit at the gallery. She decided to give her a call.

She went into the living room and sat down on the sofa, and she saw her phone on the end table where she had left it charging last night. Picking it up, she unplugged it and woke it up. She saw the little icons at the top, informing her she had Facebook notifications. She touched the Facebook icon and watched as the app started up, figuring she could call JuleighAnn later. It was still a little early for a Saturday, anyway.

Besides the notifications, there was one personal message. She touched the Messenger icon.

It was from Parker Sage.

"Hi Kenzie. I hope you slept well. I enjoyed chatting with you last night."

Hmm. She looked at the top menu bar, and saw he was currently online.

"Hi Parker. I enjoyed it too," she typed. "It's good to hear from you again. What are you up to this morning?"

Within a minute of her message, he started typing.

"Actually, kind of an unusual morning," he replied. "I did a little modeling. My first time."

"Modeling? How exciting!"

"Not really that big a deal. Just for a local calendar. Working Men of North Carolina. I'm Mr. October."

"You mean one of those nudie calendars?" Kenzie felt her breath quicken a little at the mental image it conjured up. Then, as an afterthought, she said, "Where can I get one?"

She felt a little embarrassed, and was almost immediately sorry that she sent that, but Parker didn't seem to mind.

"No," he replied, "I wasn't naked. But just barely. I was a tad bit embarrassed at first, but it got okay. And they paid me five hundred bucks for it, which I can definitely use. Then, when they were done, Marlys, the lady directing it, gave me another check for five hundred dollars, cause she said they got so many good pictures, she wanted to use one for the cover, too."

Kenzie wasn't sure what to say. She was only *half* kidding about wanting one of the calendars, but she decided not to follow up on it. Jim would never allow it anyway. Instead, she revisited something she had wondered last night.

"Parker, I'm curious. We only have one mutual friend, and you and I have never had any contact. Why did you send me a friend request?"

"It was that saying you posted. I don't know, it just touched me somehow."

Kenzie had shared a few things last night, and she didn't remember which one he was responding to. She scrolled back through her activities on Facebook from last night.

Those who are unhappy have no need for anything in this world but people capable of giving them their attention.
- Simone Weil

That was the quote their mutual friend had responded to.

"That quote you posted really meant something to me," Parker said. "I'm not familiar with Simone Weil, and I don't know if I'm interpreting the quote properly, but it reminded me of my relationship with my wife."

"How do you mean?" Kenzie asked.

There was a pause in the typing. Almost a minute passed before he resumed.

"My wife is depressed. She's never happy, and it seems like all I'm ever doing is giving attention to her needs."

Kenzie was taken aback for a moment as she read what Parker wrote. Then she started typing her response.

"I don't think that was her meaning. I think she was promoting a sympathetic and philanthropic attitude toward the suffering of others." Kenzie paused. "However, I admit that, last night, I reacted to it much the same way you did. My husband is a very unhappy person, and he doesn't have anywhere near the reason your wife has."

"I feel like such a shit for even complaining about it," Parker wrote, "because I know it's not her fault. She saw her best friend, Kathy, get murdered three years ago, and now Lily, besides not having her friend, has post traumatic stress and depression and anxiety attacks."

"Oh my God! Parker, that's terrible! I'm so sorry."

"Yeah, and now I'm the jerk who can't handle a little dark mood, when Lily is the one who done went through that."

"It takes a lot to take care of someone like that. Or of someone with a physical ailment. I was the main caretaker of my brother before he died, and I know how hard it is on caretakers. You really have to take care of yourself, too."

"Yeah, that's what my brother said. Lily's friend, Katherine, was my brother's wife."

"God, Parker! I suddenly feel like I don't have anything to complain about!"

"No, Kenzie, each of us has our own experience, and none of them can be judged by comparing them with the experiences of others. That's something I learned from Jane, Lily's therapist. Do you feel like talking about your situation?"

Kenzie pondered it for a moment.

"I'm not even sure where to start. Jim is what some would call a control freak. He likes things just right, and things get really tense if anything goes contrary to what he wants. And I'm often the one that makes them go contrary."

"He doesn't hurt you, does he?"

"No. I mean, not physically. He never leaves a mark. But it's always there, piling up in my head."

"That's at least as bad as physical abuse. If other people don't see what he does, or any physical results from it, it can be hard to get them to understand what you're going through. You end up suffering alone."

Kenzie read his response through two or three times before replying.

"Parker, that's very insightful of you. That's exactly the way it is. I've known so few people who really get that."

"I went to a lot of therapy sessions with Lily. And a few with my brother. None of them were about the same thing you're going through, but I understand the effects of emotional trauma."

51

"Yes, you sure do." Kenzie sniffed as she felt tears in her eyes. "I can't even express the feeling of relief that comes with knowing somebody understands. I'm very glad we met."

"Almost like we met for a reason, huh?"

He followed that with a smiley. Kenzie smiled too.

The street in front of the little white clapboard house was choked with police cars, and an ambulance was wedged in among them, directly in front. EMTs rolled a gurney out the front door of the house, and a man stood aside, watching as they trundled it down the driveway and slid it into the ambulance.

On top of the gurney was a body bag.

Unaccustomed to this kind of activity, neighbors watched out their windows, some shocked at the sight of the body bag. The man looked around at the neighborhood, his face looking tired and haggard, as a police detective joined him and directed him back inside.

After the ambulance silently drove away, the man sat down on the sofa. He tried not to look into the dining room, where the blood was still puddled on the table and the floor.

"If we can get back to this, Mr. Norbert," Detective Richard Jonas said, "you say you didn't come home until 3:00 this morning. Where were you?"

"I was just out driving around," Norbert replied in a monotone. "Jenny and I had a fight and I needed to get away."

"What was the fight about?"

"It was stupid. She thought I spent too much time with my friends. I said *she* spends a lot of time with *her* friends. We went back and forth about who spends more time away." Norbert looked up at the detective. "I told you it was stupid. But it's a fight we've had before."

"So you and your wife fought regularly?"

"No, not regularly. But it was a recurring theme."

The police photographer finished taking pictures of the scene and walked through the living room. As he opened the front door and left, another man came in.

"Did you fight back?" Detective Jonas asked. He had a look of surprise on his face as he saw the man come in, but his voice gave no indication of it, nor did Norbert notice.

"Just yelling back at her. She knew what buttons to push, what made me angry. Occasionally her sarcastic remarks made me mad enough that I would yell back at her, and it would be an actual argument. But I suppose I did the same to her."

"Did your fights ever get physical?"

"No. Never."

"Now, you said you just went out driving around. Did you stop anywhere? Did anyone see you?"

"I ended up at a spot over by Falls Lake. I actually fell asleep there for a while. I go there sometimes when I need to get away from Jenny. To my knowledge, nobody saw me. I didn't *want* to see anyone. That was the point. I just wanted to be alone."

The new man in the room spoke up.

"Mr. Norbert, did you love your wife?" Norbert looked up at him.

"Yes, I did."

"Have you ever wished she were dead?"

"No," Norbert said, a surprised, almost defiant tone in his voice. "I mean sure, there were times when I thought my life would be better without her. That I would be happy if she wasn't around. But they were just thoughts. Regrets." His voice broke with emotion. "We all have those. Don't you?"

"Yeah, I do."

"Excuse me," Detective Jonas said to Norbert, and he guided the new man away. Lowering his voice, he continued. "Hunter, what the hell are you doing here?"

"I saw the breaking news coverage on TV. Thought I might be able to help."

"But Hunter, you're not on the force any longer. There's nothing you can do here."

"R.J., am I the only one who's noticed the similarities?" Hunter asked.

"What similarities?"

"The wife was tied spread eagle to the top of the dining room table, her throat hacked through with a dull knife."

R.J. rolled his eyes, then looked back at Hunter.

"Come on, Hunter. The media doesn't have those details. How do you know about it?"

"So I've still got friends. But don't you see how similar this case is to Katherine's?"

"Of course, I do. All the more reason why you shouldn't be here." Hunter started to object, but Jonas stopped him. "Look, I understand you want to catch the bastard that killed Kathy. But we don't know this *is* the same guy. And I don't want your thoughts of Katherine's murder tainting *this* investigation. It's been three years and there hasn't been another case with the same M.O."

"Until now!"

"You're not on the case!"

"I *can* be," Hunter said in a tone that almost dared opposition.

Jonas rolled his eyes and looked away for a moment, thinking. He looked back and shook his head.

"Alright, Hunter. I know you're a PI now, and I know you well enough to know you won't let go. You'll keep working this case even if it's entirely on your own." Hunter raised his eyebrows and nodded. Jonas sighed. "It's against my better judgment, but I'll do this, just because you're my friend. I know the chief won't let us officially work the case together, but I'll share what I find with you, if you do the same."

"Deal!" Hunter said with a smile. "So, whaddya got?"

"Well, not much yet," Jonas said somewhat defensively. "But don't forget your part of the bargain."

"I won't. But I just got here, so I don't have anything yet."

Jonas shook his head again, flipping back through his notes. "God, Hunter, you're a pain in the ass."

"Oh come on," Hunter replied. "At the end of the day, I'm just a really great guy."

"Yeah, right. I'm not seeing that."

Hunter shrugged. "It's not the end of the day yet."

Try to be good, okay?" JuleighAnn raised her eyebrows, look-ing every bit like a scolding mother, as she held Arden's gaze. He looked up at her from his chair and put his book down in-dignantly.

"I'm always good," he replied. JuleighAnn turned her head slightly so she could look at Arden from the corner of her eyes. "What?" Arden protested.

"Not everybody gets your scathing humor."

"Listen, young lady, I'm very well aware of my mastery of the gift of smartassery. I only use my powers for good."

Seeing the futility of engaging further, she sighed and shook her head.

"Could you put Molson out back, please?" she asked. "He can be a little overwhelming when people first come in."

"I live to serve only you, my love," Arden said as he pushed himself up. Before JuleighAnn could walk away, Arden grabbed her hand and pulled her back and into his arms, planting a kiss on her lips that defied the sarcastic disregard he had just displayed.

As he held her, he pulled away from her just enough to see her face.

"You know I'm crazy about you, don't you?" he asked. Ju-leighAnn smiled and nodded, her green eyes sparkling mischie-vously.

"I kinda like you, too," she said. Her hand slipped down his back and she grabbed his ass, pulling him harder against her. She closed the space between them and kissed him back, opening her mouth to welcome his tongue. As he kissed her, she could feel a physical change taking place in Arden's midsection.

She smiled as she continued the kiss and pressed her groin against his, rubbing back and forth, grinding against him, teasing him. Then she pulled away, attempting to act nonchalant, as if the kiss and the pelvic press had no effect on her. A glance at the burgeoning bulge in the front of Arden's jeans showed quite the opposite effect on him, though.

"Later," JuleighAnn said.

Arden stood there with an almost disoriented look on his face.

"We may have to cut this visit short," he said with a deep sigh.

"In her hour of need," JuleighAnn said with mock severity, "you want to just toss her out on her ass?"

"Well, unless you think she might want to join us."

"Take Molson out back. Maybe you should stay out there with him." And her eyebrows went up again. Arden smiled and called Molson.

The golden retriever came bounding over at the mention of his name. As the back door opened, the dog shot out onto the deck, looking excitedly all around to determine what was going on in his domain. Until the door closed, leaving him alone. The excitement drained from Molson's face as he looked up at Arden through the glass door, and nearly broke Arden's heart.

"You're such a weenie," Arden muttered to himself.

"Who's a weenie?" JuleighAnn asked. Arden turned, surprised that he hadn't heard her, or Kenzie, approach behind him. He smiled and shook his head.

"Sorry, I didn't hear you sneaking up behind me."

"Guess you should turn up your hearing aid," JuleighAnn said with a grin.

"Hi Kenzie," Arden said, shaking her hand and ignoring JuleighAnn. "Good to see you again."

"Thanks. You too, Arden." She seemed a little nervous, but she looked out the glass door toward the lake surrounded by the summer foliage, and she sighed. "God, I love coming here. I don't see enough of this."

They decided to sit on the deck, which caused Molson's excitement to instantly resume. Conversely, Kenzie seemed to relax in a matter of minutes, even before JuleighAnn set glasses of her white wine sangria on the table for each of them. But Kenzie's nervousness returned about fifteen minutes later, after the small talk, when she got to the point of her visit.

"I spend so much time trying to think about what I've done," Kenzie said, "to determine if what Jim says has some validity. Maybe I *am* making him crazy; maybe I *should* try to go to bed when he does; maybe I *should* let him go through all my mail." Both JuleighAnn and Arden were shaking their heads. "I know," Kenzie continued, "I know that's stupid."

"It's easy to do," Arden said. "I lived with a crazy maker for years myself. You start second guessing everything you do or say."

"By the time I get to that point, I realize it's ridiculous and *he's* just making *me* crazy."

"The fact you realize that is good," JuleighAnn said. "You're not thinking that you're entirely to blame, or that you can't do anything right."

"Just out of curiosity," Arden said, then he hesitated. "And feel free to tell me to fuck off and to mind my own business, but why are you still with him? I stayed with Evelyn for my daughter, whether or not that was the right thing to do. But you don't have kids."

"No, not yet," Kenzie said. "But Jim has been hinting it's about time we started." She sighed. "I don't know. I've thought

59

about it occasionally, but I can't really figure it out. A lot of times, I don't even know if I *want* to leave him. I do still love him, or at least I think I do. Even though he's not quite the man I thought he was when I married him.

"But talking to JuleighAnn about it in the past has helped me to isolate some possibilities. For one thing, my dad was always really controlling, and didn't treat my mom well. At the time, it was what I knew, and I guess it just seemed normal. And I suppose, subconsciously, that's what I went for.

"And there's also some fear in there. Fear of the unknown, fear of being alone, even fear I might not be able to take care of my financial needs on my own."

"Fear of Jim?" Arden asked.

"No, not really. He's never physically abused me." She smiled a fleeting smile. "It's funny, somebody asked me about that this morning. I met a guy through Facebook, and we just kind of clicked. We chatted for quite a while."

Arden and JuleighAnn exchanged a look, and Kenzie didn't miss it.

"No, it's not like that," she added quickly. "Both he and I are married."

"So was I," Arden said as he took JuleighAnn's hand. JuleighAnn smiled at him, and then turned her attention back to Kenzie.

"We're certainly not encouraging you to leave Jim, or to start a relationship with a man you met online. Yes, it worked for us, but our situation was certainly – " she paused as if she were casting about for the right word, and she glanced at Arden again. "It was unique. But you need to analyze your own situation and determine the best course of action for yourself."

"Of course," Kenzie said, nodding her head, "I understand. And I didn't expect you to tell me what to do. I guess I just wanted reassurance that I hadn't become a terrible wife."

"Oh, no honey, I know you haven't," JuleighAnn said. "I've seen you with Jim, how conciliatory and accommodating you are to him. To be completely honest, there've been a couple of times that *I've* wanted to punch him in the face."

Kenzie smiled and looked surprised.

"Mind you, that's not a *professional* observation," JuleighAnn quickly added with a laugh.

Kenzie seemed to feel more relaxed now, and at ease. She leaned back in her chair and looked out on the lake, at various groupings of ducks and geese, at the redwing blackbirds darting among the cattails, and she sighed. Then she looked over at Arden.

"You sure lucked out in this situation," she said with a somewhat envious smile.

"Yes, I did," he replied as he looked at JuleighAnn.

"No," Kenzie said, "I mean yes, you and JuleighAnn are great together. But I'm talking about this place."

"Well, yeah," Arden conceded, "it's nice. But it's just a structure. Yes, it's a lovely house in a beautiful location, but that's not what makes it home." And he smiled at JuleighAnn.

He didn't notice the tear in Kenzie's eye.

Mason Dodd cursed his weakness. If only he had been stronger, he would still be on schedule, and he would be closer to getting out of this town. Now, everything had to be delayed. He would have to lay low for a while, stay out of sight.

All because of that damn hair!

Mason slouched down in the musty chair and put his head back. The drab little shit hole apartment barely impinged on his consciousness, but still he closed his eyes. Usually when he did that, the past would play out before him, the events in his life that led him here running in his own private screening. Those events were not all pleasant by any means, but he hoped that seeing them now might help him regain his focus.

His earliest memories were little more than vague feelings. Scattered moods connected with visual landmarks. Hazy bits of happiness against a background of the Arizona desert. Then an intangible uneasiness that swirled with the rippling waves of heat rising from the ground in the high plains of western Kansas. The uneasiness morphed into sadness when his father died, and was buried in a moldy old graveyard in St. Louis.

Due to their nomadic and sometimes vagrant lifestyle, Mason had never been given the opportunity to put down roots. Moving was just a part of life, an ordeal to be endured two, three or more times every year. Possessions were kept to a minimum, to facilitate a hasty move. Friendships were a luxury that could never be cultivated.

Oddly, though, Mason's mother, Sonya, seemed to make friends wherever they went. Ultimately, these friends would be left behind with their next move, but while Mason and Sonya were in any particular location, there was no shortage of visitors. A few would even spend the night.

Mason seldom cared for them, and sometimes even Sonya seemed fairly indifferent. But the men would usually leave in the night, and in the morning, Sonya would be in a better mood, often counting money.

Mason didn't notice the gradual change in his mother, not until he was around ten years old. At that point, he realized that Sonya wasn't the caring, maternal creature that he remembered. The realization occurred to him when they were living in a hovel in the Bronx. Both of the buildings that flanked their own were nothing but burned out shells, and the building they lived in could only have been improved upon itself by a little gasoline and a match. It was only a matter of time till it joined its neighbors.

For a while, Mason had been shivering in his bed, the two blankets on top of him inadequate to the task of keeping him warm on this frigid February morning. He could hear a faint whistle, as the wind found its way through the taped cracks in the window. He climbed out of bed, wrapping one of the blankets around him. The worn wooden floors felt like ice on his bare feet, and he walked cautiously, careful to not drag them. He had gotten some nasty splinters that way in the past.

He opened the door to his mother's room to get in bed with her, as he sometimes did when he was cold, or when he woke up from a bad dream. As he looked in his mother's room, though, he wondered if he might still be in a dream.

Sonya was naked on her bed, on her hands and knees, a leather collar around her neck. Attached to the collar was what looked like a leash, held in the teeth of the naked man on his knees behind her. His left hand was gripping Sonya's left hip as he repeatedly thrust violently into her, occasionally swatting her with the paddle he held in his right hand.

Mason recognized the paddle. It was the one that Sonya would use on him when he was disobedient. Having him lean over the edge of the dining room table, she would deliver two or three swats with the paddle.

With each slap of skin on skin, Sonya's head was pulled back a little more by the leash, her blonde hair swinging into her face, her breasts flapping fiercely back and forth. They were both grunting rhythmically with their efforts.

Mason stood frozen in place, no longer aware of the cold, as he watched the strange spectacle in front of him. After a few seconds, although it seemed like longer, Sonya noticed Mason watching.

"Mason, you little fuck," she snapped, "get the hell out of here!"

The man looked in his direction and grinned, but never missed a beat.

"Mom?" Mason said, his voice sounding more like a croak.

"Holy shit!" she spat in disgust, as she pushed the man back. She started to get up but was pulled back by the leash, still gripped between the man's teeth. Sonya turned and yanked the leash out of his mouth, which startled him, and he put a hand up to his mouth, but he pulled out of her and sat back.

"Oh, come on, Sonya, I'm almost there," the man said. She ignored him as she got up, but Mason's eyes were glued to the man's penis. He had never seen a man's erect penis before, and he was a little frightened by the size of it. The man started stroking it as he waited for Sonya.

But then Mason's view of it was blocked, first by Sonya's naked body, then by the door as she slammed it.

"Sorry," he heard her say through the door. "Just my stupid kid."

"I didn't mind," came the man's muffled voice. "He could have joined us for all I care."

"You're sick, Freddy," Sonya replied, and Mason could hear the faint slapping sound resume.

He went back to his room and took the blanket on the bed and folded it in half. Then he did the same with the blanket that was wrapped around him, and put it on top of the other one. They covered a smaller area now, but as Mason curled up under the four layers of blankets, he started feeling a little warmer, even as he was chilled by the memory of what he had seen.

"You know the routine," Sonya said, holding the paddle in her hand. Mason looked up at her, trying to keep his lip from quivering. "Come on, I've told you not to come in my room when I have someone with me."

Mason turned toward the dining room table and leaned over it. He put his shoulders down and stretched his arms out, gripping the edge of the table with each hand, waiting.

The explosive sound of the first swat made him jump, as at the same moment the shock of the sudden pain took his breath away. Even through his jeans, it felt as if his buttocks were on fire. His fingers tightened their grip on the edge of the table and he squeezed his eyes closed. The second swat was initially painful, but after that, he could feel the tingling as numbness began to set in.

He heard the clatter of the paddle on the table beside him as Sonya put it down.

"That's all," she said. "Just remember what I told you."

Mason pushed himself up and nodded.

He turned to look at her, but she was already walking out of the room. Mason picked up the paddle as he now allowed the tears to flow down his face.

Leaving the dining room, he walked back toward Sonya's bedroom, feeling with each step the sting of his underwear and jeans as they rubbed against the burning skin of his butt. He placed the paddle on Sonya's bedside table, trying not to look at the rumpled sheets, or remember the scene he had witnessed there a few hours before.

hank you for this," Kathy said. "I guess I just needed to talk about it." She pushed her plate a couple of inches away and pulled her iced tea closer, taking a drink. She looked around at the crowd in the Chili's restaurant. Then she looked back at Lily and smiled in embarrassment. "It was all just so stupid."

"Most fights are," Lily agreed.

It was three years ago, but Lily remembered the conversation vividly. Every word Kathy had said. Every expression that crossed her face. Every nuance of vocal inflection.

"Hunter was a cop before I met him. It's part of who he is." Kathy sighed and shook her head. "I was just so childish. I wanted us to be able to spend Labor Day together. And I had such big plans."

"That secluded picnic idea you mentioned sounds so nice," Lily said.

"Oh, more than nice," Kathy said, and she leaned closer against the table and lowered her voice. "I got some sexy lingerie from Victoria's Secret. I was going to wear it under my hiking shorts. When we got to the picnic site, I was going to strip for him and make love to him right there."

"You?" Lily gasped, her eyes wide.

"I know. He's always wanted to have sex outside and I was always afraid. What if somebody sees us? What if we get caught?"

"I know. You've told me."

"This was kind of a big deal for me. But I figured as secluded as this place is, it would be safe."

"You can still do it. Just some other time."

"I know, but I had my courage all worked up for today. But that's the thing. I know his schedule can change quickly, and sometimes without notice. I know it's not his fault he had to work on a holiday."

"No," Lily said, "and you also know it doesn't mean he loves you any less. Hunter adores you."

"I know." Kathy traced her finger down the side of her glass, pondering the smooth streak through the beads of condensation. She looked back up at Lily. "And I've always hated the idea of starting the day with an argument. I mean he's a cop, for God's sake! What if something happened to him, and his last memory of me was of me being angry at him?"

"Don't worry, honey," Lily said, placing a hand on Kathy's. "Nothing's going to happen to Hunter."

"I know, Lil. I try not to think about it, but he *is* a cop. That possibility is there every day."

"Yeah, but if you think too much about it, you're just going to make yourself depressed." Lily looked out the window. "Come on, it's a beautiful, sunny day. Let's go out and enjoy it."

"What do you want to do?" Kathy asked, and she took another drink of iced tea.

"I don't know, let's just go out and walk around. See if anything comes to us." Lily looked askance at Kathy. "I know I'm not Hunter, but maybe you can try to have a good time with me anyway, huh?"

"I always have a good time with you," Kathy smiled. "You know that."

"I promise I won't make you strip for me."

"Oh, well thank you for that," Kathy laughed.

"So come on, then! Let's get out there!"

70

"Well, let me finish my tea!" Kathy slurped the last of it up her straw. "God, what was in your quesadillas?"

"I just don't want to waste a beautiful day." Lily quickly figured a twenty percent tip, signed the charge slip, and put it back on the little tray that the waitress had left. Grabbing her purse, she slid out of the booth and stood there waiting for Kathy.

Kathy rolled her eyes and picked up her purse with a sigh of mock frustration. She slid out of the booth and Lily grabbed her arm. They walked toward the door, their golden blonde and fiery auburn hair swinging back and forth in unison.

Parker took two bottles of Olde Hickory Appalachian Ale from the refrigerator. In the time it took him to get the bottle opener, the bottles were already coated with condensation. After prying off the tops, he handed one bottle to Hunter.

They carried them out the back door to the covered patio and sat down in the cushioned wrought iron chairs. It was September. The day had been warm, but it was beginning to cool off in the evenings. They clinked the bottle necks together and drank, each downing half their bottles.

"Oh damn, that helps," Hunter said, putting his head back.

"Yeah? Hard day?" Parker asked.

"Frustrating day." Hunter rubbed his eyes with his knuckles. "You know about this case I'm working on."

"That murder similar to Kathy's?"

"Yup. I'm kind of working with an old buddy. We've been interviewing people, going over the crime scene with the proverbial fine-toothed comb. There's just nothing. No clues, no fingerprints, no physical evidence of any kind. Not even a strand of hair that shouldn't be there."

"A strand of hair?" Parker asked incredulously, looking at Hunter.

"Yeah. Cops vacuumed the whole house and examined the contents of the vacuum cleaner bag. So far, every fiber, every hair, everything that was found can be accounted for."

"God, what a shitty job!"

"Gotta be done. And usually it gives us something. Anything, however small, that we can follow up on. A fiber from a piece of clothing that's not in the closet, a hair that belongs to somebody who isn't in their circle. But there's just nothing."

"Maybe it was somebody who *is* in their circle."

"We're considering that. In fact, the husband is a pretty good suspect. He was alone at the time. No witnesses, no alibi."

Something in Hunter's voice made Parker turn to him.

"But you don't think so?"

It was a few seconds before Hunter spoke. Parker noticed he was scratching the scars on his wrists again.

"I don't think so," Hunter finally said. He sat quiet for several more seconds, then he shook his head. "Everybody grieves differently, but still I recognize his behavior. Three years ago, I went through what he's going through. His remorse is real."

He allowed another pause, then sighed and looked at Parker.

"Which means we got nothing."

"Sorry, Hunt, that sucks."

"I couldn't believe my luck at first. I had just started looking into Kathy's case when I got a call about this latest murder, Jenny Norbert. I mean, obviously it's not so great for the Norberts, but as far as catching this psycho, I thought we were getting somewhere. That we could put this guy away and maybe I could have a little closure. Lily, too."

Parker puffed out his cheeks as he blew, making a frustrated sound. Hunter looked over at him.

"How's it going, little brother?" he asked.

Parker shook his head. He glanced back at the house, then leaned toward Hunter and spoke quietly.

"I don't know what more to do for her. The medications don't seem to be enough, or the right ones, or the right combination, or

74

whatever. In the meantime, she's going crazy and she's taking me with her."

"Shit," Hunter said under his breath. "I was hoping I could gently pick her brain, see if she might be able to remember anything that might have lain dormant since Kathy's murder."

"Huh," Parker scoffed. "I don't see that happening."

"I need to get a better description of this guy. 'Average height, average build, no face?' Obviously her subconscious is suppressing it, but I hoped maybe we could bring a little more to the surface."

"Sorry, man."

"Well, it was a thought."

Parker heard a soft shuffling sound and turned toward the back door. He thought he might have seen Lily's shadow moving from the door, but he couldn't be sure.

ily's cries filled the room, and Parker was awake in a moment, the sound ringing in his ears. Not quite screams, the sound echoed against the walls, pounding back against them, almost as if it was amplified in the dark.

Parker turned toward Lily and gathered her in his arms. She struggled, pushing against his chest, but he held her tight.

"It's okay, honey," he whispered. "It was just a dream. You're okay."

Lily's cries turned to a sustained wailing, which went on for a few minutes. Parker continued holding her, rocking back and forth in bed in a motion that, early on, he found soothed her.

"It's okay, baby, you're okay," Parker kept whispering, until the wails turned to deep sobs. By this time, as was her pattern, she was so weakened by all the energy expended in the screams and crying, that she finally relaxed again.

Parker loosened his hold on her, but continued rocking, until her sobs gradually stopped, and he could hear her sleeping again. He gently slipped his arm out from under her neck, and Lily settled herself into her pillow.

He rolled back over on his side of the bed and looked at the clock. He hadn't been asleep long. It was only one o'clock. He lay on his back, trying to relax, but his whole body was a knot. He sighed. He wouldn't be falling asleep any time soon.

Parker shook his head and got up. The windows were open and the room was cool, but beads of sweat dotted his forehead.

He hunched up his shoulders, tilted his head both directions and stretched his arms, but every muscle still tingled as if a low-voltage current was pulsing through them. His nerves were on edge.

He softly closed the bedroom door behind him and walked into the kitchen, squinting as he turned on the light. After a few seconds, he could open his eyes in a squint, and he walked toward a cabinet. He took the bottle of bourbon down and poured a swallow into a glass. He tossed it back, and as he leaned against the counter, he felt the heat work its way downward, and his body began to relax. Another deep sigh and he stood upright again, replacing the bourbon in the cabinet.

He rubbed his eyes as he walked through the dining room and into the family room. He didn't bother to turn on a light. There was enough light from the kitchen to see by, and as he looked around, he realized this was probably about as dim as it was in here most days when he was gone. He knew that Lily kept the blinds and curtains closed during the day. She opened them before he got home, but he had heard from different neighbors they were usually closed.

Parker sat down heavily on the sofa, and he picked up his cell phone from the coffee table. As long as he was up. . . .

He touched the Facebook icon, watching the familiar blue screen. As soon as it had started up, he saw there was a private message for him. He touched the Messenger icon, then Kenzie's name. He smiled when he saw she was online. It was only eleven o'clock in Denver.

"Hey you," he typed, "you're up."

"I was just about to go to bed," Kenzie replied. "What are you doing up so late?"

"Lily woke up with another one of her night terrors."

"Oh, I'm sorry. So you won't be going back to sleep for a while."

"No, I don't think so."

After they started communicating by private message a couple of weeks ago, Parker had described these attacks to Kenzie, and their frequency, usually two or three a month. Labor Day had been bad. He had kept Lily sedated for practically the whole weekend.

"I don't think I can take much more of this," Parker said.

"Honey, I'm so sorry," Kenzie responded. Terms of endearment had begun slipping into their conversations during the past week. By a mutual agreement, they both said that the other was welcome to vent about their circumstances whenever necessary, a prerogative they each took advantage of regularly.

Kenzie had, just the night before, cried on Parker's virtual shoulder about an hour-long badgering she had endured from Jim about the dinner she had made. Not only was it late, but the orange roughy was a little overdone and tough.

She didn't blame Jim for not liking it. She didn't care that much for it, either. But she had gotten away from work about ten minutes later than usual, which got her meal preparations started later. Then she had underestimated the time to steam the asparagus and was distracted by that, leaving the fish under the broiler a couple of minutes too long.

Being home before her, she knew that Jim could have helped out with dinner preparations. She also knew better than to suggest it.

As Parker and Kenzie's venting to each other became commonplace, so did their sympathy, followed by their terms of endearment.

"What triggered this one?" Kenzie asked.

"My brother, Hunter, was over this evening. He was talking to me about a case he's working on. Another murder similar to Katherine's. I think Lily might have overheard part of the conversation."

"Oh, no. Are they close to catching the killer?"

"They got nothing. No clues at all. Anyway, I guess Lily went to sleep with all that in her mind and woke up screaming."

"The poor thing."

"I know," Parker sighed as he typed, "I feel sorry for her too. But I don't think I can take this anymore. She ain't getting any better, and she's dragging me down."

"What are you going to do?"

Parker sat still for a few moments, pondering. The thoughts had been there for a couple of weeks now, but he had not come anywhere near a decision.

"Not entirely sure," he typed, "but I think I need to get out before she drives me crazy."

"You said her parents could care for her. Have you talked to them?"

"No I haven't, but I know I gotta protect myself. It kinda scares me, though."

"Why?"

"Well, like I've said before, I feel like a total shit for even considering leaving her in this condition. And I'm sure friends and neighbors will look at me that way, too. I guess it's silly, but I don't like people thinking bad of me. I like for people to think I'm a good guy."

"Aw, honey, you ARE a good guy. But you do have to take care of yourself, too."

"Yeah, that's what Hunter's been telling me."

"You want to know something crazy?" Kenzie asked. "I've been considering leaving Jim."

Parker sat up and reread the message slowly, to be sure he had read it correctly. He turned the words over and over in his head. His mind was racing now.

"Really, sweetie?" he typed. "What got you thinking about that?"

"It had entered my mind on other occasions in the past, but I started thinking seriously about it a couple of weeks ago, when I was talking with some friends."

"Have you made any kind of decision?"

"Not yet, but every time Jim badgers and criticizes and insults me, it pushes me a little closer to the door." There was a pause, then she started typing again. "What do you think?"

Parker sat there looking at the display on his phone, trying to put into words what he thought.

"I think you should leave him and come out here," he finally typed.

Leave Jim and move to North Carolina? Kenzie stared at the sentence. The idea of leaving Jim was not the hard part. Of course she hadn't been able to work up the courage to do it yet, but it wasn't a foreign idea by any means. Moving to North Carolina, however, that was a hard concept to accept.

And why would she go there, anyway? What would draw her to the south, of all places? There was obvious attraction between her and Parker, but did it go deeper than that? Their private chats in Facebook Messenger were comfortable. They related well to each other, mutually sympathetic about the others' situation, for sure, but even when the conversations were not about problems, they just enjoyed each others' company.

The terms of endearment they had begun using just came naturally, and neither of them had questioned it. Why? Were they just friendly nicknames, or were they a sign of stronger feelings?

"Why do you think that?" she finally asked. Then she waited, intently watching her phone, for Parker's response to appear. It took a little time.

"I been thinking about us lately," he replied. "I know we've only known each other for a couple of weeks, but Kenzie, we're good together."

Pretty much what she expected to see. What surprised her was the feeling of agreement, and the warmth she felt inside when she read it.

But . . . .

"Parker, the south just doesn't appeal to me. I tried to explain that when we first met and practically swallowed my foot whole."

"I know," he replied, "but we talked about that. We ain't the hillbilly capital you thought we were."

For the second time, the 'ain't' grated on her nerves. She imagined what he must sound like, but looking at his handsome smiling face, she had a hard time reconciling the hick, backwoods sound that came to mind.

"I remember you mentioned Duck Dynasty," Parker continued. "But they're in Louisiana, not North Carolina. You mentioned Honey Boo Boo. They're in Georgia. Here near Raleigh and Durham, it's nice. Progressive cities, beautiful hills and dense forests."

"But the heat and humidity, Parker. I think that would drive me nuts!"

"You get used to it. I don't think it's that bad, but when it does get too hot, just stay inside. We got real air conditioners here too, you know." Kenzie smiled.

"I'm sure you're right. I'm sure it's probably just my silly preconceived notions about the south."

"So come on out," Parker pleaded.

"I can't do that, Parker. A cross-country move like that would be really expensive. I don't have any money."

"But you work full-time."

"I do, but my pay is deposited into our joint account, and Jim handles the expenses. He allots a certain amount of money for groceries and gas. If I need to buy something, clothing, shoes, anything like that, I need to arrange it with him."

"Baby, do you realize how fucking archaic that is?" Parker wrote back. "It's your money, money that you worked for and earned. But you have to ask him for it?"

"I know. I've known that for a while. But there's nothing I can do about it without making him angry or rousing his suspicion."

During this exchange, Kenzie began to notice something interesting. A feeling of excitement that she hadn't felt in a long time. A fluttering feeling around her heart.

"Why don't you come here?" she typed, surprising herself.

"I have a business here, honey," he replied. "I got obligations. I can't just pick up and leave."

Of course. She knew that even before he replied, but it was still a disappointment to see it.

"I understand. I guess we're stuck. For now, anyway."

She could hardly believe she had tears in her eyes.

Mason Dodd sat at his computer looking up news stories from local archives. Something caught his eye and he picked up a pen and scratched on a pad of paper, adding to his already copious notes. His computer was old and slow, with the cheapest dial-up connection available. And he could barely afford that. He knew just enough about the computer and the internet to be able to find what he was looking for, but it was a long and arduous process.

Just yesterday, he had decided to take some positive action instead of just sitting around on his ass. He thought about going to the library, but he didn't want to risk somebody seeing what he was doing and spoiling his plan. Odds were quite slim that anybody would figure it out, but he just didn't want to take the chance. So he found an old used computer for sale in the classifieds that he figured he could manage if he cut back on food for a while. His dishwashing job didn't pay much.

Mason's biggest worry was that his money would run out before his mission was complete. His financial situation was never great, but it had never been stretched this tight. Even after his father died and it was just him and his mother, Sonya, he had never had to skip a meal.

When Sonya decided it was time to move on, they left the dilapidated building in the Bronx and moved upstate for a few months. During the next couple of years, they meandered through eastern Pennsylvania before ending up not far from where they had been, but in a comparatively better apartment, in Trenton, New Jersey. And thus began a new parade of 'friends.' One in particular would make an impression on Mason.

Sonya had cleaned herself up and got a part-time job as a sales clerk at JCPenney. One sweltering evening in August, she brought a co-worker home with her.

"Mason, say hi to Monica," she said as she came in the door. Mason was sprawled on the sofa struggling through some homework, but he quickly sat up when Monica walked in.

She appeared to be in her late twenties, a few years younger than Sonya. Mason thought Monica's features were a little rough, but attractive. Certainly eye-catching. Her hair was black. Really black, he thought, like comic book characters whose hair is drawn with blue highlights. Her lips were full, slightly parted, with red lipstick. And she had the lightest blue eyes he had ever seen.

She came into the apartment fanning herself with one hand, and with a jacket draped over her other arm. The tight tank top she was wearing, without a bra, would not have been acceptable on the sales floor at Penney's, so she had worn a blazer over it, but she had taken it off the moment she left.

"Hi, Mason," Monica said in a sexy, sandpapery voice.

"Hi," he managed to say.

"Make yourself at home," Sonya said before disappearing into the kitchen.

Monica smiled at Mason. Her eyes quickly swept the apartment, then settled back on Mason. Besides the tight tank top, she was also wearing slip-on wedge sandals and a light cotton skirt, and Mason caught himself looking frequently at her impossibly long legs.

Mason was a good-looking towheaded kid. At thirteen, he was big for his age, looking a couple of years older, but completely confounded by the hormones coursing through his veins. In only a few seconds, Monica noticed his infatuation and started playing with it like a new toy.

She plopped down in the chair opposite Mason, sighing loudly. She slipped off her shoes and stretched her legs straight out in front of her.

"Damn, it's hot!" she said, and began flipping her skirt to fan her legs, at the same time displaying her white lace panties with each flip.

Mason began to feel the heat too.

Monica watched Mason's face as she continued fanning her skirt, and Mason watched her, seeing that she fully intended for him to see. When he squirmed to accommodate his growing erection, Monica smiled and stopped.

"What are you working on there?" she asked. Mason didn't have any idea what he was working on, and had to look back down at his homework.

"M- uh, math," he stammered. Mercifully, Sonya came back in the living room with two tall glasses.

"Here's a Vodka Collins for you, my dear," she said.

"Thank you!" Monica said as she took the glass and drank a couple of swallows. Sonya sat down in the love seat, which was at right angles to Monica and Mason. "Oh, I needed this," Monica said, and she put her head back as she placed the cold glass against her chest, reveling in the coolness.

Watching her, Mason was almost surprised that her hardening nipples didn't actually rip through the fabric of her tank top. He tried to direct his attention back to his homework, but he looked back up when Monica sputtered.

"What's wrong?" Sonya asked.

"Mason doesn't know what to make of me," Monica replied with a smile. Sonya looked at Mason with a confused expression, then back at Monica. Monica touched the glass directly to her nipples, further sharpening their contours. An added effect was the condensation wetting the light colored fabric, and Mason could clearly see the pinkish brown areolas around her nipples.

Mason was trying not to hyperventilate, and his mother snorted a laugh.

"Mason, what's wrong with you?" she asked. "For heaven's sake, you've seen me completely naked before, and even having sex."

Monica sucked in a quick breath.

"He's seen you having sex?"

"A few times. Not the whole thing, but he's walked in on me when I was with someone."

Mason tried to focus his attention back on his homework as they continued talking about him as if he wasn't there. But as time passed and more alcohol was consumed, they became more difficult to ignore. Mason thought about going to his room to finish, but he stayed where he was. Despite his embarrassment, he was fascinated by Monica and her blatant sexuality.

"Have you ever made love to a woman?" Monica asked. Mason looked up at her and shyly shook his head. "No, not you," she replied with a laugh, "I was talking to your mom."

Sonya nearly choked on her drink and slapped her hand over her mouth and nose, trying to swallow as she laughed at the joke. Monica laughed at her, which made it worse. After nearly half a minute, Sonya was able to swallow and she took a breath. Then she cleared her throat and looked at Monica.

"No, I haven't," she said.

"Huh?" Monica asked, looking confused.

"Made love to a woman."

Monica's eyes widened as she smiled and got up a little unsteadily from her chair and sat next to Sonya on the love seat.

"Honey, I think it's about time!" Monica slurred.

"Why?" Sonya asked. "You know, I never understood the attraction. You have the same equipment as I do."

"Oh, but nobody knows what a woman likes better than a woman!" To underscore her point, Monica slipped her hand under Sonya's blouse and started doing something with her breast. Startled, Sonya pressed herself deep into the back of the love seat and grasped Monica's hand through her blouse. It appeared that she fully intended to protest, but whatever Monica was doing to Sonya's breast, she made her point quickly.

Sonya's breathing quickened and a slight smile appeared on her lips. She looked at Monica briefly, her smile spreading a little wider, before she relaxed and let go of Monica's hand, putting her head against the back of the love seat.

Mason could see the shape of Sonya's bra under her blouse, bunched up above her breasts, though he couldn't tell exactly what Monica was doing. But his erection was back with a vengeance!

Monica started kissing Sonya and continued fondling her breast. Sonya, already amenable to this new experience, reached an arm around Monica's back, pulling her closer. With her other hand, she pushed Monica's tank top up and began fondling her nipples, oblivious now of Mason on the sofa.

Mason had never seen two women making love. The sight of these two kissing and groping just a few feet away from him was arousing him more than he had ever been. He kept watching, quietly lest they remember that he was there, as they each pulled off the other's blouse. Monica reached around and unfastened Sonya's bra and removed it, all without breaking the connection of their lips and tongues.

Mason watched wide-eyed as they resumed kissing and caressing. He didn't even realize he was stroking himself through his jeans. But when Monica leaned over and licked Sonya's nipple, he realized in an instant what was about to happen. In a panic, he jumped up from the sofa, one hand tightly gripping his crotch, and made a dash for the bathroom.

Sonya and Monica briefly looked up, surprised, then laughed and resumed their lovemaking.

Parker arrived home, pulling his Silverado under the carport, next to Lily's Corolla. She almost never drove it anymore. In the last three years, he could count on one hand the times she went someplace on her own. Still, Parker made a point of keeping it maintained and licensed.

That's not what caught his attention now, though.

Hunter's Impala was parked in the driveway behind Lily's car. Parker wasn't aware Hunter was coming over. In fact, Parker hadn't planned on being home now himself. He had planned on going to The Sawmill with Bud and Joe after work, but Bud had decided he wanted to go straight home. He and Shelly were trying to work things out and he was spending more time with her lately. At that, Joe decided that he was pretty tired and just wanted to go home, too.

Parker picked up his lunch box from the seat beside him and went in the side door of the house, which led into the kitchen. He put his lunch box on the counter and continued through the dining room, where he saw Hunter's blazer draped over the back of a chair. He went into the family room at the back of the house.

Hunter was sitting on the sofa, his hand on Lily's. Lily was crying softly.

"What's going on here?" Parker asked.

"Parker!" Lily said as she looked up at him, clearly surprised, wiping the tears from her face. She looked, oddly, at the windows. "I'm sorry, I forgot to open the blinds."

"I don't care about the damn blinds," he replied. "What's this about?"

Hunter placed a reassuring hand on Lily's arm as he got up and walked toward Parker.

"I apologize, little brother," Hunter said quietly. "I thought I'd just give it a try, to see if Lily could think of anything that might help with the case."

"Are you out of your fucking mind?" Parker hissed as he grabbed Hunter by the shoulder and propelled him toward the dining room.

"Now, take it easy, Boo," Hunter said.

"Don't 'Boo' me! I'm not five anymore." Parker angrily slapped the light switch on.

"No, you're not," Hunter said, squinting. "I know that. I'm sorry. But like I said, I thought it was worth a try." Hunter leaned back against the table.

"Don't lean on the table!" Parker said. Hunter quickly pulled himself away from it.

"Sorry. You still haven't fixed that?" he said with a grin. "You're a carpenter, for God's sake!"

"I've been busy," Parker snapped, unfazed by Hunter's smile. "But what about Lily, man? You know what she's like. You know what those memories do to her."

"I know it's hard for her," Hunter said calmly. "But I figured if I just questioned her gently, it might pay off."

"Pay off?" Parker echoed angrily. "You're gambling with Lily's mental health! That ain't something you can just toss out on a table and hope your luck holds out!"

"No, bro, it ain't gambling. I've picked up a thing or two from my sessions with Dr. Jeffries. I just wanted to try to gently guide her thoughts to see if she could remember anything she hadn't related before. Some detail that might have been submerged for the last three years."

"You know *why* those details are submerged?" Parker asked. "You know what remembering that day does to her?"

"Yeah, I do. I also know what allowing that psycho to roam the streets did to Jenny Norbert."

"Sounds like you're blaming Lily for that."

"No, Park, I'm not blaming her at all." Hunter's tone was still calm but firm. "But you know how badly I want to put this son of a bitch out of commission. You know how invested I am in this. This is *not* just another case."

Parker sighed and rubbed his hand across his face.

"I know, man. I know how much you lost, too." He looked up at Hunter. "Lily was a mess on Labor Day. I just don't want a repeat of that."

"Yeah, well I didn't do too good myself," Hunter said softly.

"What do you mean?"

Hunter was silent for a few moments, rubbing his eyes with his knuckles. He looked back at Parker.

"I was in pretty bad shape on Labor Day too. My gun and I spent a few hours having ourselves a heart to heart." He paused again, then he shrugged. "I ain't too sure which one of us won, but I'm still here."

"Hunter!" Parker said alarmed, but trying to keep his voice quiet, for Lily's sake. "Holy shit, man, why the hell didn't you call me?"

"Because I knew you would already have your hands more than full with Lily, and I didn't want to take you away from her. She needed you more than I did."

"What if you'd gone through with it?"

"But I didn't."

"You couldn't have known that early on, though. I could have lost my brother that day. And do you know what that would have done to Lily?"

Hunter turned and leaned against the back of a chair.

"Ultimately, that's what kept me from doing it," he said. "Knowing how it would affect Lily. That, and the knowledge that Kathy's killer would still be out there."

"Damn!" Parker said under his breath. He reached out and put a hand on Hunter's shoulder. "I'm sorry, man. Is everything okay now?"

"No, everything is not okay," Hunter said as he looked up at Parker with tears in his eyes. "That bastard's still out there doing the same thing he did to Kathy. I mean to put a stop to that."

Parker sighed and nodded.

"So, were you able to learn anything new from Lily?"

Hunter shook his head and rubbed away the tears.

"No. If she does know anything we don't, she's got it buried too deep." He looked back at Parker. "I'm sorry I went behind your back. I was just in the neighborhood and I thought of it. But I should have checked with you first."

"I'm sorry she couldn't help you."

They were quiet for a few moments. The quiet was interrupted by Lily.

"Parker?" she said softly. Parker quickly turned to see her squinting at him in the light of the dining room. "I want to help if I can."

I t was late on a grey Saturday afternoon. Kenzie lay in bed panting, squeezing her nipples, trying hard not to disappoint Jim. He was busy down between her legs, working her clitoris with his tongue and slipping a finger in and out, caressing the front wall of her vagina. Kenzie was wet and quivering, but despite all Jim's efforts, and her own, in the last twenty minutes, it just wasn't going to happen.

This was their time to make love. Every Saturday afternoon, whether they needed to or not. It might as well have been written on the calendar, because it just worked best with Jim's schedule. Unfortunately it didn't always work best for Kenzie.

"Jim," she said, "I don't think I'm going to cum." Jim stopped his efforts and looked up at her between her breasts. She met his disappointed gaze and gave a shrug. "I'm sorry, honey. It felt good, but I guess I just can't loosen up enough."

Jim sighed and gave her inner thigh a kiss. Without a word, he moved upward, kissing her nipple on the way, and inserted his penis in her vagina. He finished the job for himself in a couple of minutes. He kept thrusting into her until the spasms ended, then he pulled out and rolled over on his back, his chest heaving from the effort.

Kenzie remained quiet for a few seconds, lying beside him as he caught his breath. Then Jim patted her thigh and got up, going into the bathroom. He had a routine for after-sex cleanup, too, and Kenzie waited, listening. After a minute or so, she heard the toilet flush. When she heard the water start running in the sink, she got up and knocked lightly on the door. Jim opened it and she went in.

"I think I'm going to take a shower," she said. Jim nodded and continued his cleanup. Kenzie adjusted the water for her shower and got in under the spray.

She was just reaching for the shampoo when she heard Jim's voice, though she couldn't make out what he said. She slid the shower door open a bit and stuck her head out, pushing her wet hair out of her face.

"What?" she asked. Jim was standing there, still naked, holding a blister pack of birth control pills.

"Why are you taking these?" he repeated.

"I don't understand." She felt the beginnings of a knot in her belly. "Those are the same ones I've been taking for months, now."

"Why are you *still* taking them?"

"Why would I stop?" She pressed her eyebrows together as she looked at him in confusion.

"We've talked about it."

"Yes, but we hadn't come to a decision, yet."

"I thought you wanted to have kids," Jim said, the tension in his voice building.

"I do, Jim, someday."

"Someday? You're thirty-one. What the fuck are you waiting for?"

"Can we talk about this after my shower?"

"No! I'm pissed *now.*"

Kenzie sighed as she turned and shut off the water. Then she stuck her head back out the door, self-consciously positioning her naked body behind the door.

"Jim, I'm sorry. I didn't think we had actually made a final decision, so I just kept taking them."

"It's *not* that there was no decision made," Jim said angrily, and he started emphasizing key words in each sentence. "We've had *several* discussions about it. You know *exactly* how I feel. But you don't give a *shit* about it!" For added emphasis, he pounded his fist on the counter.

By now, Kenzie was in a standing version of a fetal position – her head was inclined a bit, her eyes down, her legs pressed tightly together, her knees bent, her arms clenched against her chest, and still positioned behind the shower door. More a psychological response to Jim's anger than a reaction to the cool air on her wet skin, though she felt that too.

She looked up at Jim who was just standing there looking at her. She wasn't sure if he expected a response, but she didn't know what to say. He glared at her for a few seconds, his face reddening, a vein in his forehead throbbing. Then he made an angry hissing sound as he threw the blister pack on the counter and stomped out of the bathroom, slamming the door behind him.

Kenzie softly closed the shower door and tried to take a deep breath. She was surprised at how shallow her deep breath was. She reached down to the knob and turned the water back on. For a second, it was cold, which shocked her and caused a sudden deeper intake of breath, but then it quickly warmed up to its previous temperature.

She stepped closer to the nozzle, allowing the water to spray on her face and over her head, immediately washing away the tears that were coming.

It was quiet as Kenzie padded softly down the stairs. She made the circuit of the house, but Jim wasn't there. Then, in the kitchen, she saw the note, scrawled in an angry hand.

Out with Rick. I'll be late.

Kenzie felt the relief wash over her. She knew it wasn't over. But at least she had a reprieve for the evening.

She went into the living room and collapsed on the sofa, pulling her wavy red tresses in front of her, over her shoulder. She knew Jim hated it when she leaned back against her wet hair and left damp spots on the furniture.

She sat motionless for a while, not relaxed, just inert. Barely breathing, barely blinking, she stared blankly ahead for several minutes, concentrating on breathing. Thinking about previous conversations with Parker, she finally reached for her phone. She started up her Google maps app and typed "Englewood, Colorado." A map of her approximate location appeared. She touched the "Route" link in the upper right, then typed "Allure, North Carolina."

She knew it was a pretty good distance, but she didn't realize just how far.

"1,684 miles. 23 hours, 28 minutes without traffic."

Shit.

She still felt her preconceived prejudices against the south, but she had come to feel as if it might not be so bad. At least Parker was there. But it's not as if moving there had even been possible before. However, seeing that number, 1,684, just seemed to further reinforce the bars of her cage. Like it or not, she was trapped. Even if she could bring herself to leave Jim, there was no way she could get to North Carolina.

She started up Facebook and logged in. Since she started chatting with Parker, she made it a point to log out of Facebook when she wasn't using it, rather than just quitting the app. She didn't want to take the chance that Jim might open it up and see their conversations.

A quick glance at the Messenger window, and she saw that Parker was not online, though he had left a message for her.

"Hi, baby. I sure miss you."

98

Those six words were enough to loosen her tense muscles, and she felt the chill melting away, something that her shower had not quite accomplished.

"I miss you too, honey," she typed. She knew it was about 7:30 in North Carolina. She didn't know what Parker would be doing now, but moments after she sent her message, he was online.

"Hi sweetheart," he replied.

"Wow," Kenzie typed. "Talk about good timing!"

"My phone vibrated to let me know I got a message. How are you doing?"

"Kinda bummed. Jim and I had a fight. The whole baby subject again."

"Oh, I'm sorry. Wanna talk about it?"

"Not really. Same old thing. But he's now gone for the evening. How about Lily?"

"She's asleep. Her meds, and the depression itself, make her really tired. So she's usually in bed by seven or seven thirty."

"To top it all off," Kenzie continued, "I'm even more bummed because I went to Google Maps and found the distance between you and me. 1,684 miles!"

"Damn! That sucks."

"No shit. And it feels especially far now."

She paused for a moment, nervous to continue. What she was feeling now was a new development, or at least a new realization.

"Parker, I just want to feel your arms around me, and to hear you tell me everything's alright." She sighed. "I really want you now!"

Some time passed as she watched her display, nervous that she had gone too far. Then she saw that he started typing.

"Baby, I been wanting you for a while, too," he said. "But I didn't know if I should say anything."

Kenzie slowly let out the breath she hadn't realized she had been holding.

"I been wanting to hold you," he continued, "to run my fingers through that incredible hair of yours, and feel your body against mine."

Kenzie felt almost like crying again, and she noticed that she was breathing freely once more. Able to draw deep breaths into her lungs, she felt herself relaxing.

With the relaxation came a feeling, a longing, a warmth, deep inside. If only she had felt that about an hour ago, when Jim was between her legs.

And she smiled as she imagined Parker looking up at her from there.

Her name is Kenzie Stewart," Parker said. He had stopped at Hunter's house after work. He felt like talking to someone, but for some reason, he didn't feel like talking to Bud or Joe about it. Parker and Hunter were in Hunter's living room, Hunter in his usual spot on the love seat, and Parker in the armchair across from him. "We've been chatting for a few weeks. It's kind of freaky, because we've never met." The volume of his voice dropped a little in a tone of wonder. "But I think we might be falling in love, man."

"Damn, little brother," Hunter said, "you didn't waste any time!"

"I know. It's crazy!"

Parker got his phone and opened Facebook, then opened Kenzie's profile. He quickly found one of his favorite pictures of her. She was outside, in front of the gallery where she worked, at the opening of an exhibit. He had seen other photos from the same event, with the owners of the gallery, her co-workers, and with the couple whose work was being exhibited. But this photo was of Kenzie by herself.

Her thick, wavy, red hair cascaded around her face, complimented perfectly by the bricks of the building behind her. Her fair skin glowed in the early evening light, and her eyes, usually a warm brown, blazed now with happiness, and with the light of the setting sun. Her smile was relaxed, not forced, and Parker found himself smiling when he looked at her.

He handed his phone across to his brother. Hunter took the phone and after his initial glimpse of the picture, he whistled. He looked at it for several seconds, studying her face. He looked up at Parker with one eyebrow raised, and he handed the phone back to him.

"She's beautiful," Hunter said. "And she's married?"

"Yeah," Parker replied, looking at the picture a few moments longer, as if he was unwilling to tear his eyes away. "Unhappily. Her husband's a fucking asshole. Treats her like shit."

"Have you decided what to do about Lily?"

Parker looked up at him and sighed, then looked back down at his phone and shut down Facebook.

"No," he said, his voice reflecting the reluctance he felt at discussing it. "I know what you've told me, and it makes perfect sense. But I just can't get past the idea of people thinking *I'm* a fucking asshole."

Hunter looked at him, now with both eyebrows raised.

"I know," Parker said, exasperated. He looked down at his hands clasping his phone, and he sighed. He looked back up at Hunter for a few moments before continuing. "I know it sounds like a cliché, but growing up, I was always in your shadow."

"My shadow?" Hunter exclaimed. "I was an absolute terror growing up! Black sheep of the family. I drove Mom and Dad crazy. They were more surprised than anyone when I joined the police academy."

"I know," Parker agreed.

"So how were you in my shadow? It ain't like I set the bar very high for you."

"That's what I mean, Hunt. You were always the bad brother. I heard some of the shit people said about you, and the way they said it. I didn't want them to talk about me like that."

Hunter scoffed.

"And here I thought you admired me."

"I *always* admired you," Parker said with a wistful smile. "And I secretly wanted to be like you. But I just didn't have it in me. You got the rebellious smartass gene. I got the shy people-pleaser gene. So to think about our friends and neighbors thinking I'm a royal shit, well that whole idea just drives me crazy."

"Parker, the problem's not going to go away just because you don't like to think about it."

"I know."

"A few weeks ago, I asked you if you still loved Lily. You said you didn't know. Have you come up with an answer since then?"

"I want to," Parker sighed. "Love her, I mean. I did before, but she just ain't the same person she was."

"Neither am I."

"Well no, of course not. But damn, Hunter, at least you're functional!"

"It's one of my greatest accomplishments."

"See, that's what I'm talking about. You can still be a smartass. Lily doesn't have a sense of humor anymore. I don't even think she knows how to smile."

"Well think about it, little brother. That day was the worst for both of us. We both lost Kathy that day. We both retreated into our own darkness. Within a few days, I tried to kill myself. Just be thankful Lily's not suicidal."

"I am, Hunter. But look at you now. You came through it."

"Mostly, yes. But the big difference between Lily and me is that, while we both lost Kathy that day, Lily was there and saw it happen."

Parker looked at Hunter and nodded.

"I know. I know it's hard for her. I know she sees that every day. And honestly, I sympathize with her." Parker paused and shook his head. "But I don't know if I can ever feel for her the way I did before."

"Well, Parker," Hunter said softly, leaning forward, "you owe it to her to make a decision. You gotta make a move. If you don't love her anymore, don't draw it out."

Trenton, New Jersey became the closest thing to a real home that Mason Dodd ever remembered. Sonya seemed to like it there. Months passed and she still hadn't gotten the urge to pack up and move on. Monica was a big part of the attraction for her.

And for Mason.

In the middle of June, 1994, he was fourteen, still big for his age, and just out of junior high school. Without school to go to, morning came a little later, but Mason was still usually the first one up.

He was pouring Frosted Flakes into a bowl when, from behind him, he suddenly heard "Ha!" and felt hands grip his waist, in an effort to startle him.

"Do you have to do that every morning, Monica?" he asked, clearly unfazed.

"I *don't* do it every morning," she replied indignantly as she came around to his side and leaned against his shoulder. "I'm not here every morning." She got a bowl for herself and, while she waited for him to finish pouring the milk, she leaned against his shoulder again, this time in an effort to push him off balance. Mason pushed back.

"You're worse than a sister," he said.

"Oh, but I'm also *better* than a sister," she replied, and she grabbed his neck and pulled him toward her, planting a kiss on his lips. "What sister would do that?"

Mason looked at Monica, feeling a little flustered, as he so often did with her. Without makeup, her face was rather plain. Her features were fairly average, except for her light blue eyes. But he liked her full sensuous lips and her quick smile, and the way she talked to him as a grown-up. True, some of that talk was mocking or sarcastic, but she talked the same way to Sonya, sometimes. Monica made Mason feel like an equal, and that made her beautiful in his eyes.

He also liked her blatant sexuality, and her propensity for walking around the apartment wearing nothing but a t-shirt, like she was now. She had great legs and proudly showed them off. A couple of times, Mason had even seen her completely naked. That made her appealing to him in other ways.

He smiled at her and, without a word, picked up his bowl of cereal and went into the living room. He seldom ate in the dining room. That was still usually the place for meting out punishment and he didn't feel comfortable sitting there. Though Mason was about the same size as Sonya, and he was usually a good kid, he still occasionally received a paddling there.

The love seat directly faced the TV, so it was much more conducive to a pleasant meal. He sat down there and turned on the TV. A moment later, Monica carried her own bowl of cereal in and sat next to him.

Bryant Gumbel and Katie Couric were excited. They were debuting their "window on the world," the glass-backed Today Show set. Now, people on the street could stand and gawk at them as they reported on a shooting in Spokane, Washington and the surrender of O.J. Simpson after his bizarre low-speed chase a couple of days before.

It was just background noise, though. Monica had put her feet up on the coffee table, next to Mason's, and kept pushing against them, or pressing her knee against his, in order to gain more space on the coffee table for herself. It probably would have been extremely annoying to Mason if she wasn't half naked and if he wasn't fourteen.

As they were eating their cereal and playing footsie, they heard a shuffling sound from the kitchen. They looked up as Sonya peeked around the doorway.

"Monica, you fucking slut," she said, "how many times do I have to tell you to stop making out with my kid?"

Monica puckered up her lips and made a noisy kiss in her direction. Sonya smiled at her and retreated back to the kitchen to make a cup of tea, while Monica drank the milk from her bowl. Then, as she lifted her feet off the coffee table, the bottom of her t-shirt flipped up momentarily, proving to Mason once again that jet black was not her natural hair color. Unconcerned, she got up and disappeared in the kitchen, taking her empty bowl with her.

Mason stayed there, watching Bryant Gumbel and Katie Couric, now outside the studio, interacting with the crowd on the sidewalk. As wonderful as their window on the world was, apparently it didn't give them quite enough contact with the outside world.

Mason wasn't really paying attention to the show, so it was easy to shift his attention to what Sonya and Monica were talking about as they came back in the living room.

"I'm just saying we could make some good money," Monica said.

"I do okay," Sonya replied. "I make more than enough to live on, combined with the part time job at Sears." She had left the job at Penney's a few months before, though Mason didn't know the details. He knew that Monica didn't work there anymore either. She now worked in some sex toys shop.

"I'm talking about better than okay," Monica said.

They both settled on the sofa as the Today Show cast was now reminiscing about Barbara Walters' history with the show. Monica pulled one foot up on the sofa in front of her and wrapped an arm around her leg, oblivious again to Mason, as she continued.

"Yeah, you have two or three guys a week, on the nights I'm not here. And like you said, you do okay. But what if we teamed up? Lots of guys fantasize about two women at once!"

"I've never done a threesome," Sonya said, taking a sip of tea. "I wouldn't know what to focus on."

"All we have to do is start making out ourselves. The guy will get horny watching us and want to join in. Then we just play off of him. But think how much more we could charge for that!"

"How much are you talking about?" Sonya asked.

"I don't know, but I know of at least one dominatrix who charges almost a thousand bucks an hour!"

"Shit!" Sonya pondered. Then she touched Monica's knee. "Put your leg down, honey. You're going to give Mason another boner."

Monica looked at Mason, who tried to look as if he was watching the Today Show. She smiled and put her foot down on the floor.

"So how would we get this started?" Sonya asked.

"I get questions about it now and then at work. I'll see what I can find out."

On a Tuesday evening, Parker came home from work to an empty house. Lily had called him earlier that day to say that Hunter was taking her out to the neighborhood where Kathy's murder had taken place, to see if he could trigger any memories. Parker was concerned about it, but Lily assured him that, even though she was concerned as well, Hunter was going to keep a close eye on her and would get her away at the first sign of trouble. Parker had reluctantly agreed.

Without Lily to monopolize his time, Parker thought he might tackle an item or two on his to do list. Turning on the kitchen light, though, he was distracted when he saw that a small, flat parcel had come for him. Lily had put it, along with the rest of the mail, on the little kitchen table, where they usually ate dinner. Seeing the usual assortment of bills and junk, he picked up the parcel instead. He took a steak knife from the cutlery holder on the counter to slash through the packing tape, and he opened the box. Inside was a short stack of calendars. Ten copies to give out to friends.

And there was Parker, smiling on the cover in a cropped shot, showing his face and chest, his hands behind his head. 'Just like a professional model,' he thought.

He flipped through the calendar, casually glancing at the other men. There was a lawyer, a cop, a welder, and of course the requisite fireman, each with a short paragraph about them. He got to October and found the full-length shot of himself, holding four

2x4s on his shoulder. Parker was smiling at the camera, his dimples deep and sharply defined in the morning light, his skin glistening.

And just like Marlys had said, it looked almost as if the tool belt and his boots were the only things he was wearing. Despite the embarrassment he remembered feeling, he had to admit, he looked pretty damn sexy.

In the box, along with the calendars, was a business card. North Ridge Promotions, Raleigh, North Carolina, Marlys Rosenfeldt, Vice President.

Parker got out his phone and called the second number on the card. It was after six o'clock, and he figured the office would be closed now. The second number was probably her direct line or cell phone. Marlys answered on the second ring.

"Hey, Marlys," he said with a grin. "It's Mr. October."

"Hi, Parker. How you doing, son?" she asked in her deep, lusty voice.

"Doing great! I just got the calendars. Thank you."

"You're very welcome. Spread them around. I see big things in your future. I'm actually glad you called. I was wondering if I could meet you sometime in the next few days. I may have some more work for you."

"Really? Uh," he thought for a moment, "yeah, I could meet you on Saturday."

"Great. Saturday afternoon would work for me. Are you familiar with the Club Carolina, off Capital Boulevard?"

"Never been there, but I know of it."

"How does one o'clock sound? They have a great menu. We can have some lunch and talk about this new project."

"One o'clock, Saturday. I'll be there."

"Great!" Marlys enthused. "And Parker, it's starting to look like I might be able to keep you busy for a while. If you're interested."

Parker Sage, professional model, he thought as he disconnected. He smiled and put his phone in his pocket, and he looked up as he heard the front door open.

He was expecting the worst as he came out toward the entry. It wasn't the worst, but it didn't look good. Hunter was holding Lily, supporting her with his left arm, as he closed the door behind them. Lily was pale, more pale than usual. Her eyes looked a little glazed and distant. Her breathing was shallow and fast, but steady.

All those signs registered with Parker in a glance, and he rushed toward them.

"She's okay," Hunter said reassuringly. As confirmation, Lily looked at Parker and nodded.

"I'll be fine, honey," she said softly. Parker took her from Hunter and helped her toward the family room, but she stopped at the hallway. "I think I just want to go to bed," she said. "I took a Rhotrimine a few minutes ago, and I'm getting kind of sleepy." She kissed his cheek and pulled away. "I'll be fine. Really," she said again as she walked a little unsteadily down the hallway toward their bedroom.

Parker watched until she disappeared into their room. Then he turned toward Hunter.

"I am not happy about this, man," he said quietly.

"Sorry, Park," Hunter replied, "but she insisted she wanted to do it. She really did great, considering."

Parker looked at him for a moment, then sighed.

"So? How did it go?"

Hunter shrugged and shook his head.

"Nothing new," he said. "She was able to relate to me details that she remembered as we drove around. But none of it was anything that isn't already in the case file."

"Still no description of the guy?"

"No," Hunter replied bitterly. "Still no face."

"Hmm," Parker said as he looked worriedly down the hall. Then he looked back at Hunter. "Well, I'm sorry it didn't work out. But I guess it was worth a try."

"Yeah well, we're not giving up," Hunter replied. "We're going to try again in a couple of days."

"What? Again? Why?"

"To try to find out what she knows. What she's locked away. To see if I can find who did this to her."

"To her?" Parker's voice registered disbelief. "I thought you were doing this for Kathy."

"Kathy's dead, Park. Yes, I want to get the guy that killed her. That's the primary thing that's been driving me for a while." Hunter paused as he glanced toward the hallway where he had last seen Lily a couple of minutes before. "But as you know, he's the same guy that did this to Lily. And I happen to think there's a chance that little girl might still be saved."

"But you saw what this did to her today. What do you hope to accomplish by taking her out there again?"

"What I hope, little brother, is that in the course of this, we might dig up something that leads me to the killer. Whether it happens or not, I can't really say. But as long as Lily's willing to try, so am I."

"This is just going to drive her over the edge." Parker said.

"What do you care?" Hunter said, lowering his voice to a hiss. "You don't love her anymore. You've been wanting out of this anyway."

"Not like this!" Parker lowered his own voice to match Hunter's. He nervously paced back and forth a few steps. "If I leave Lily after she gets even worse, I'll look like an even bigger shit than before."

"Damn it, Parker, you *look* like a man. Why don't you *act* like one?"

Parker stopped and looked at Hunter.

"What the hell are you doing, Hunter?"

"Trying to catch my wife's killer."

"Bullshit! You just said you're doing this for Lily." Parker squinted at him, thinking. "You've been making me think I should leave her."

"I have *not* been telling you to leave her," Hunter shot back at him. Then, remembering Lily in the other room, he lowered his voice again. "You're the one who's been lamenting that you don't love her anymore. You're the one who *wants* to leave her, but is too worried about what everybody will think. You're the one who wants to hook up with that little lady in Denver. I've just been telling you to be a man and make a decision one way or the other."

Parker studied Hunter for a moment.

"Are you sure you're not just trying to get me out of the way?"

"Get you out of the way?"

"I think you've got a thing for Lily, but don't want to make a move while I'm still here."

Hunter closed his eyes and sighed. Then he opened them again and looked hard at Parker.

"Parker, I love Lily," he said. "She's your wife. My sister-in-law. Kathy's best friend. I love her like she's my own sister. I want to catch the bastard who killed Kathy, and who left Lily like this. And that's what I intend to do."

Parker just stared at Hunter, trying to decide if he believed him. Hunter didn't wait for a reply.

"Well, listen, I know you still got your panties in a twist about me. I can't help your unfortunate lingerie situation. But I'm not going to let anything happen to Lily in the process of my tracking down the killer." He walked past Parker, patting his shoulder on his way out. "I got shit to do. I'll talk to you later."

113

The sun was blazing overhead. Lily and Kathy felt the heat from above, and radiating off the asphalt, as they carried their bags from the shopping center.

"Why don't we head over to the park?" Lily asked, keeping her face inclined toward the sun as they walked through the parking lot. "Suthern Cumfort is playing a free Labor Day concert at the band shell." Suthern Cumfort was a popular local band that played in a lot of local venues – mainly bars and clubs. Lily was crazy about them.

"You and your Suthern Cumfort," Kathy replied with a smile. "You know, if you weren't already married to Mr. Universe, I'd think you had the hots for someone in the band."

"Oh, look who's talking," Lily protested. "I've seen you go nuts about their music too."

"Yeah, but I wasn't talking about their music."

Lily grinned back at her, and they were silent for a few steps.

"No," Lily finally said, "I'm pretty happy with my catch."

"I know you are, honey," Kathy said. "In fact, I think we both made pretty good catches out of the gene pool."

Lily smiled at her. "So?" she said. "You want to go to the park?"

"Sure, why not," Kathy said in a tone of mock surrender.

At the mall, they had spent a couple of hours shopping. Retail therapy always made them feel better, and they each carried a couple of bags containing their plunder. Lily saw that Kathy was in a noticeably better mood when she popped the trunk on her car. They deposited their bags and closed it, then Kathy pressed the unlock button on her remote twice, to unlock the doors on both sides.

They had both gotten in and closed their doors when the back door on Kathy's side opened. Alarmed, they both turned around as a man with no face slid in the back seat and closed the door. Before either of them could voice a protest, they saw the gun in his hand.

"Start up the car," the man said.

They sat paralyzed, trying to remember what they should do in such situations.

"I don't have a problem with killing either one of you," the man said in response to her hesitation. "So I suggest you do as you're told."

"Kath," Lily said shakily, "maybe we should just take him where he wants to go?" She didn't mean it as a question, but that's the way it came out.

Kathy nodded stiffly and started up the car. The man directed them out of the parking lot, and in minutes, they were heading west on Spring Forest Road. Kathy's eyes darted back and forth, unblinking, as she followed the man's directions, her knuckles white as she gripped the wheel.

Eventually, they found themselves on a twisting road in an upscale residential neighborhood, thickly forested with maple trees.

"Turn left here," the man said.

"Where are you taking us?" Lily asked, turning around to look at him.

The faceless man responded by raising the pistol and pressing the muzzle against her forehead. Lily closed her eyes and held her breath. She heard Kathy whimper as she made the turn. When no shot was fired, Lily opened her eyes again. The man pulled the gun back, and Lily turned to face front, slowly letting out her breath.

Following the winding road, the man directed them to make a couple more turns. The houses were set back from the road and spaced far apart, with trees between them and in front of them. Lily nervously noted how private the setting was.

"Turn in this driveway on the right," the man said.

Kathy turned and they saw the garage door rising, revealing an open space.

"Kathy," Lily said in a quietly warning tone.

"Better do as you're told, Kathy," the man said. "Pull into the garage, or I'll put a bullet in Blondie here."

Lily noticed that tears had left streaks down Kathy's face, as she pulled into the open space in the garage. The garage wasn't empty. The other space was occupied by an old rusty brown Dodge Dart, circa 1975. Not what they would have expected in this neighborhood.

Once they were fully in the garage, the man clicked a button on the remote in his hand, and the door began cranking back down. Lily looked back as the garage door slowly descended, blocking the daylight, and the outside world, from her sight.

Lily opened her eyes. It was dark. She looked around and recognized her bedroom. Her current bedroom, three years later.

She realized she had only been dreaming about that last day with Kathy. But for the first time in three years, she didn't wake up screaming.

She sat up in bed, thinking, remembering. She wiped away the tears that her memories of Kathy brought, then she reached for the phone.

117

've dreamed about you the last three nights!" Kenzie said with a tone of amazement. She was sitting in her living room with her computer on her lap. She was looking at Parker on her screen, as they spoke to each other on Skype. It was after nine o'clock and Jim was asleep. Even so, she was talking quietly. "I'm going crazy imagining you touching me."

"Honey, I think about touching you all the time," Parker replied. "Holding you. Making love to you."

Kenzie sighed.

"You don't mind that?" Parker asked. "Being made love to by a southern boy?"

"No, Parker, I don't mind at all." She snickered. "In fact, hearing you talk now, I've decided I like your voice, your accent. You kind of sound like Elvis Presley."

"Well, thank you very much, ma'am," he said, sounding *very much* like Elvis Presley. He even imitated the sneer.

Kenzie snorted, then slapped her hand over her mouth.

"Ha," Parker exclaimed, "I love that you snort when you laugh."

"I don't always," she replied. "You just caught me off guard."

They were quiet for a few moments, listening to each other breathe.

"This is so weird," Parker finally said, "being able to talk to you, to see your face, to hear your voice." He sighed. "And knowing that my wife is asleep in the other room."

119

"I know. And my husband's asleep upstairs."

"If only things could have been different," Parker lamented, "and we could have met a few years earlier."

"Yeah," Kenzie replied, echoing his sigh. She looked at Parker's face for a few moments. "Well, this sure changed fast."

"What do you mean?"

"That brief moment of levity quickly turned back into these feelings of longing and regret."

"I got plenty of that!"

"Have you decided what you're going to do?" Kenzie asked. "About Lily, I mean?"

"Not for certain, but I'm pretty sure I'm going to call it quits."

"Really?" Kenzie replied breathlessly.

"Pretty sure. It just ain't working with us."

Kenzie felt an odd mixture of emotions knotted around her heart.

"You're not doing it just because of me, are you?"

"What do you mean?"

"I don't know," Kenzie said, frowning. "I just have this feeling that I might have contributed to that. I don't want to be a home wrecker."

"No, baby," Parker drawled. "My marriage was in the shithouse before I ever met you."

"You don't think the timing of this decision is suspicious?"

"Well, there's been no decision yet. I ain't a hundred percent certain, but I think I been trying to work up the nerve to do it for a while now."

"And you're saying that I'm helping you work up the nerve?"

"No. Actually, Hunter's the one who's been trying to get me to decide. You just give me something to look forward to when I finally do." Kenzie smiled and felt the knots loosen. "If you'd just hurry up and get out here." And the knots tightened back up just a little bit.

"Parker, you're forgetting, there are 1,684 miles between us."

"No, I ain't forgetting. It's just some driving."

"Honey, I seriously don't know how I can do that."

"How much do you think it would cost?"

"I don't have any idea," she said, thinking about it. "It's twenty-four hours of driving. With just me driving, I won't have anybody to switch off with. I'd probably have to break it up into about three days. So it would take enough gas to drive 1,684 miles, plus motel rooms and food."

"Okay," Parker said decisively, with a nod of his head. "I been thinking about this. I didn't tell Lily about that second check I got for the calendar cover. Think you can get here on five hundred dollars?"

"Well," Kenzie replied, hesitantly, "yeah, maybe."

"Good. I'm going to send you this money. I want to help you get out here."

"Parker, no," she protested, "you don't have to do that."

"I know I don't have to," he replied. "I want to. I love you, Kenzie."

Kenzie caught her breath when she heard the words, and she felt a shiver ripple up her spine. She had been thinking the same thing, but this was the first time that either of them had put it into words.

"I love you too, Parker," she said softly. She loved the sound of it, and she felt that shiver radiate outwards through her body. But then, she fought to remain realistic. "Okay, so let's say you send me the money and I have enough to drive out there. What then? What do I do once I get out there?"

"You just let me worry about that part. I'll make arrangements for us."

Kenzie's mind was racing. Could she do it? Could she actually leave Jim? Strike out on her own and go to an unfamiliar part of the country?

To be with someone she's never actually met?

"I'm going to have to think about this," she said.

"That's fine, babe. You do that. In the meantime, give me your address and I'll send you a check."

"Okay, you can send it. I won't say yet that I'll definitely use it, but you can send it. Just don't send it to my home. Jim's usually home before me and gets the mail. I'll give you my work address."

As she recited the address to him, she felt a strange fluttering feeling inside her.

She just couldn't determine if the flutter was good or bad.

Mason looked at himself in the mirror. He was wearing black leather pants, criss-crossed with zippers and straps and buckles, and a jacket to match. It was Monica's idea. She had enlisted his help tonight as they embarked on their first threesome job.

"It's important to create a mood," she had said when she brought the outfit from work, "a mystique. So you can be our maître d'."

"I don't understand," Mason had said. "What do I need to do?"

"Just greet the man at the door, take his jacket if he's wearing one, and lead him to us. We'll be in the bedroom getting warmed up." She had grinned and walked away at the time.

Now, as he was in full gear, Monica came back, looking him over, as his mother prepared the bedroom. Mason was distracted from his own outfit when he saw Monica.

She was rocking the black leather and lace, starting with six inch stiletto heels and fishnet stockings, attached to a garter belt. Above that was a leather-trimmed g-string with a sheer lace insert. Finally, she had a leather trimmed bra with no cups, topped with more sheer lace in the form of a camisole.

Her glossy black hair was parted in the middle, cascading down both sides of her face and over her shoulders. And all but hidden by the hair were her pale blue eyes, appearing even lighter in contrast to the smoky blue-black eye shadow.

As he saw her approaching him in the mirror, Mason's breathing intensified, and his outfit became more kinetic as the pull tabs on the zippers began swinging back and forth.

God! What was it about Monica? Mason was magnetically attracted to her, drawn to her beyond words. But he was scared of her, too. He looked at her reflection beside his in the mirror. Seeing her wearing just a t-shirt, well obviously that was sexy. But this – this was almost more than he could take.

"Nice," Monica said as she looked him up and down. "Very nice! Sexy." She played with the buckles and the chunky zippers. The pull tabs on the zippers were two inches long and all the hardware was shiny silver. The outfit really was dripping with bits of metal. Monica was fingering all of it. Before he knew it, she pulled the one at the fly. Mason felt the pants loosen at his crotch and he jumped, startled.

"Oops," Monica said with a smile and an expression of mock surprise, and she pulled it back up. But the vibrations of the hefty zipper traveling down his penis and then very slowly back up, at Monica's hand, was enough to shatter the remnants of the calm he had struggled to establish.

"Don't worry, babe," she said, slapping his butt, and keeping her hand there, "you look great."

Mason looked back at his own reflection. Focus, damn it! He took a deep breath.

"I look like Edward Scissorhands," he replied, striving to regain the tenuous calm.

"Ha!" Monica laughed. "He looked great, too."

Mason noticed that Monica's hand was still on his ass, and he turned toward her. Inches away from her, he looked her in the eyes, feeling the quickening of his breathing again. She smiled at him. Not her usual smartass smile, but a real one, a sweet smile. He looked down at her breasts, her nipples clearly visible through the sheer lace.

Tentatively, Mason reached up and touched one, glancing back up at her face. Monica was still smiling, and he became a little bolder, grasping her breast in his hand. It was softer than he had expected, though the nipple itself was firm.

His pants, already tight, had grown tighter. Not accustomed to such snug clothing, he could feel a throbbing as his hard-on was struggling to grow in its confined space. Monica's smile faded and her lips parted slightly as she looked up at him, her eyelids lowered to cover nearly half her pale blue irises. Mason had never kissed a girl before, and he wasn't sure if this was an invitation or not.

He leaned forward slightly, waiting to see her reaction. He was surprised when her reaction involved putting her other hand on his crotch. She felt how hard he was and she smiled again. Mason put his arms around her and kissed her full on the lips. When her tongue entered his mouth, he was momentarily shocked, but then he accepted it eagerly.

While his mouth was busy on hers, his hands were clumsily exploring her body, one hand on her back under the lace camisole, the other on her bare ass. Her hand was still on his cock, and in just a few seconds, he felt the pressure building to a familiar conclusion. Embarrassed, he tried to pull away, but her other hand, still on his butt, held him in place.

Mason was panting as Monica held him until the spasms were over.

"I'm sorry," he said, a mortified expression on his face.

"Don't be," Monica replied, her voice quiet but still husky. "It's okay," she smiled. "It happens. You're young. There's plenty of time."

Mason felt tears in his eyes as he looked at Monica, and he leaned forward and kissed her, softly this time.

They both heard a sigh and turned to see Sonya, in a skin-tight red latex body suit, standing in the doorway to the kitchen, her arms folded across her chest. Their reactions couldn't have been more different. Mason quickly looked away, completely flustered and embarrassed, while Monica sputtered in laughter.

Mason wasn't sure if she was laughing at him, or at getting caught by his mother.

He ventured another glance at Sonya. She was still standing there watching him, her eyebrows raised, just waiting for him to look back at her.

"What are you just standing there for?" she asked. "Go get the inside of those pants cleaned up. Our guy's going to be here soon."

As he headed for his bathroom, he heard Monica laugh again, but just before he turned the corner, he glimpsed the soft look she was giving him.

The city of Denver was, in general, laid out on a grid, with avenues going east and west, and streets going north and south. In the middle of that, though, was downtown Denver, which was laid out diagonally. It was a small section of the city turned about 45 degrees, roughly parallel to the South Platte River and Cherry Creek, where the original nineteenth century gold strikes were made. Larimer was a one way street, going southwest, lined with old fashioned brick storefronts.

As a chill settled over Denver in the first week of autumn, the unadorned sky was a bright blue, but the air was crisp. A light frost had formed on the ground that morning, and the leaves were starting to change color. A few were even making an early break from the trees and tumbling along the ground in the light breeze, the alternating colors of their tops and undersides flashing like runaway glitter.

Gallery BC had responded to the chill by turning the heat on. Kenzie thought it just felt stuffy, so it felt good to get outside during her lunch hour.

She had arranged for her friend, JuleighAnn Harper, to meet her for lunch. They sat on one of the green metal benches lining Larimer Street in front of the gallery, facing the traffic, their backs to the sun. They were eating Jimmy John's subs that JuleighAnn had picked up.

Kenzie was beginning to wonder if meeting JuleighAnn had been a mistake.

"Honey, I'm not saying that he's a serial killer or anything like that," JuleighAnn said. "I'm saying that you just don't know what he's really like after knowing him online for only about a month."

"But Jules," Kenzie countered, "I can judge people pretty well. I've known some people for just an hour and knew that they were bonkers. For some people, a month is more than enough time to get to know them."

"Perhaps, if you knew him in real life. But online, people can be whoever they want to be. I mean, look at the way I met Arden. He was pretending to be someone else altogether and I didn't have a clue."

"Yeah, but he came clean to you, so you knew who he really was then. And *you* only knew each other for about a week."

"Arden came clean because he's a decent person. But for every decent person online, there's a not so decent one looking to deceive someone."

Kenzie was frustrated. She had thought she would have more support from her friend. She took a bite of her sandwich and pondered what JuleighAnn had said. She wanted to honestly consider the advice her friend was giving her, but it was hard. JuleighAnn took that opportunity to take a bite of her sandwich too.

"But Parker's not deceiving me," Kenzie insisted, getting her second wind. "He's a good person stuck in a bad situation, just like me. Just like Arden was. Parker's not pretending to be someone else."

"Maybe not, but he could be showing you only part of who he is. A person can pick and choose what they show online."

"We know each other more than just online. We've talked on the phone several times. We've even Skyped a couple of times. So in a sense, we've been face to face, able to see how the other acts and reacts."

128

"That's good," JuleighAnn replied consolingly. She sounded as if she was softening a little, perhaps realizing that she had been too negative. "That's still fairly one dimensional, and without other people around. It's important to see how people act around others, but you're right, that's a start."

"And we've known each four times longer than you knew Arden," Kenzie said with an almost triumphant tone, as she wiped a little sauce from her mouth with a napkin.

"But neither Arden nor I picked up and left our familiar surroundings and our friends to move across the country to a completely unfamiliar area to be with the other."

Kenzie felt a little deflated at that.

"I don't even have many friends," she said, feeling the tears coming to her eyes. "Jim commands so much of my time and attention. We do what he says, including the time we spend with others. So my friends are mainly his friends."

"Kenzie, *I'm* your friend," JuleighAnn said.

Kenzie blinked her eyes and the tears spilled down her cheeks. She blotted her face with her napkin and sighed. She felt the steam going out of her argument, and JuleighAnn sympathized with her.

"Honey, I know you're in a bad situation. I know Jim's not a good husband, and I understand you're suffering because of it. And now you meet this young man who, I admit, is an amazing piece of eye candy. He treats you well, he makes you feel good, and you're seeing him as your salvation.

"And maybe he *is* a great guy. Maybe what you're seeing really *is* the real Parker Sage. But the fact is you just can't know that for sure yet. Not in the time and the circumstances under which you've gotten to know him."

Kenzie held the remainder of her sandwich in her hands, prone on her lap. JuleighAnn leaned toward her, pressing their shoulders together.

"If you decide that leaving Jim is the right thing to do, great," she said softly. "Move out and get an apartment in Denver. I'll be here for moral support every step of the way."

Kenzie looked at her out the corner of her eye, trying to smile, and they put their heads together for a moment.

"Thanks, Jules," she said quietly.

They were silent as they each took another bite of their respective sandwiches. Then JuleighAnn looked up at Kenzie, her eyebrows drawn together in confusion.

"I thought you didn't care for the south," she said, "or southerners, or their accents."

Kenzie made a guttural sound and laughed.

"Honey," she said with a bit of a southern accent herself, "I've changed my mind."

'm not so sure I'd call it a break in the case," Hunter said, glancing at Lily in the passenger seat. "Not that many Dodge Darts around nowadays, and this was three years ago. And we don't have a license or registration on it. But just the fact that you remembered a new detail is encouraging."

He pulled into the parking lot at the shopping center.

"Hopefully you might be able to remember something else. Like the guy's face."

Lily smiled a nervous smile. "I hope so," she said, but Hunter could already see her stiffening in her seat as he drove toward the area where she and Kathy had parked that day. He was anxious to get started, to retrace their final drive on that day three years ago, but he wanted to make it as easy for Lily as possible. He found an open parking space and pulled into it. He shifted into park, put the windows down and turned the car off. Then he turned toward Lily.

"Listen, hon, just try to relax, okay?" he said, making sure his voice was soft and soothing. "You're completely safe. You're with me. Nobody's going to hurt you. We're just going to retrace the route again. See if you remember anything."

Lily nodded and tried to take a deep breath.

"And like the last time," Hunter continued, "if it gets to be too much, you just say the word and we'll leave."

Lily looked at Hunter and nodded again. Her hands were folded in her lap, but Hunter could see that her knuckles were white and she was sitting up rigidly in her seat. Her eyes were wide, her face tense, her breathing quick and shallow.

The scars on Hunter's wrists were itching, and he had an overwhelming urge to scratch them, but he resisted. Instead, he rested his arm on the open window and sat back in his seat, trying to appear casual. It was a pleasant day, and the sun shining in the windshield was warm. He wanted Lily to relax. He looked at her and smiled.

"You remember when Kathy and I got married?" he asked.

"Of course," she replied, with the ghost of a smile on her lips.

"It was a pretty day in April. Things were just starting to get green. You and Parker were still a few months away from getting married."

Lily looked at Hunter as he reminisced. Hunter slowly rubbed his left wrist on the window and his right one on his pant leg. Talking about Kathy was calming, but it also taunted the demons that he so carefully struggled to keep confined.

"I was nervous," he continued, "but then little Minnie Thompson comes marching up the aisle carrying her basket of flowers. She had heard her musical cue and took off. Just couldn't wait for Luke Parrish to finish tying his shoe."

Lily's smile became a little more pronounced now.

"He came running up the aisle after her," she said, "carrying the rings, and forced Minnie to take his arm for the rest of the way." They both smiled at the memory.

"I was so tickled watching him try to force her hand through his arm, and still stay in step to the music that I forgot all about being nervous."

"They're both thirteen, now."

"Damn," Hunter said, shaking his head. "Well, then you started coming up the aisle."

Lily's hands were relaxing their grip on each other, and Hunter could hear her breathing becoming a little steadier.

"You just looked so pretty in that mint green dress and the little flowers in your hair that, just for a second, I wondered if maybe I had picked the wrong girl."

Tears were welling up in Lily's eyes, but she was still smiling.

"I glanced over at Parker standing there beside me, and I saw that you had pretty much the same effect on him. He just couldn't tear his eyes away from you. I smiled at him, but he never saw it.

"And then Kathy appeared and started walking towards me. I tell you, when I saw her smile at me, I just fell in love with her all over again."

"And forgot all about me, huh?" Lily said, a little stiffly, but still smiling. An attempt at humor. Hunter was encouraged.

"Kathy did win my heart," he said, smiling back at her, "but it was a close race."

They sat quietly for a few moments, lost in their own thoughts, until Lily broke the silence.

"Just a few months later, and you were standing up there beside Parker again, on the other side."

"Yeah. And seeing Kathy come up the aisle again, as *your* bridesmaid, I felt that same nervous, adoring flutter again. I'm a cop. I ain't supposed to feel nervous, adoring flutters. But she did it to me every time."

Without thinking about it, Hunter gave in and scratched his wrists.

Lily sniffed and wiped the tears from her eyes, and she looked back at Hunter. Hunter returned her gaze for a few seconds.

"'Till death do us part' came too soon," he said.

Lily nodded as her eyes filled up again. Hunter reached over and placed his hand on top of hers, squeezing lightly.

"Help me catch this bastard, okay honey?"

Lily closed her eyes, and the tears left a glistening path down both cheeks. She took a deep breath, and then blew it out, trying to will herself to relax. She looked up at Hunter again, and she nodded.

"That's my girl," he said, and he started up the car.

Thursday night, Kenzie sat on her sofa with her computer on her lap, talking to Parker again on Skype. She was watching his face intently, waiting for him to respond. Finally, he looked up at her.

"I don't know," he said, frowning, "it seems kind of silly, but sometimes I can't help but think Hunter just wants to get me out of the way, so he can have Lily."

"Has he ever expressed any interest in her?" Kenzie asked, watching Parker's face on the screen.

"Not that I've ever known. But he's just been spending a lot more time with her lately." Parker quickly nodded and continued. "I know. I know it's because he's investigating Kathy's murder. I get that. And he does seem to be getting Lily to remember things. And she's – well, she ain't enjoying it, but she ain't bothered by it as much anymore."

"Well, that's good, right?"

"Oh, sure," Parker readily replied. "It's great. I hope Hunter can catch the guy that killed Kathy."

"Are you jealous?"

Parker looked at Kenzie for a moment.

"No. I mean I don't think so. Why would I be? I don't love Lily anymore."

"Are you sure? Maybe there's still something there."

"No. She ain't Lily. Not the Lily I loved and married. I just don't feel anything for her anymore."

"Maybe you just feel bad that Hunter may be getting through to her when you couldn't."

"Yeah, maybe."

"You said she's remembering things?"

"She is. Apparently not anything that helps yet. But it's a start. They're hoping that if they keep retracing that last day, that eventually some important detail will surface."

"Oh, I hope so," Kenzie said sincerely. "I wish them the best."

"I do too," Parker agreed. "But it just hurts that he'd try to manipulate me to give Lily up so he can have her."

"Do you really think that's what he's doing? Would he do that to you?"

Parker sighed and rubbed his face.

"I don't know. Probably not. He's a good guy. I think I'm just making up shit in my head."

"Are you sure you still want to leave Lily?"

"Yes, I do. I've pretty much made up my mind on that score. I just haven't worked out the logistics yet."

"Well, if he *is* interested in Lily, I think this is kind of perfect timing."

"Yeah, Hunter kind of implied the same thing when I told him about you, too."

Parker smiled slyly at Kenzie.

"Speaking of which," he continued, "have you decided about coming out here?"

"I have," she nodded. "I've decided that I'm going to use the money you sent me, for which I am extremely grateful, to travel to North Carolina."

"Excellent!" Parker said with a full-on smile. Those dimples were so deep, they looked almost painful. "I sent it 'second day.' You should get it tomorrow."

"I'm going to use it to book a flight and I'll go out there for a visit, maybe a week."

"Wait, a visit?" he asked, as his smile faded. "And then you'll go back to Jim?"

"For now. Parker, we've known each other for just over a month. We've never even been with each other in person. We need to see if we're even compatible before I can make the decision to pick up and move out there."

"Okay," Parker replied, nodding, "fair enough. That makes sense. When will you come?"

"I don't know yet. I still need to work out the logistics, as you said. And an alibi. I've got a friend here who I'm sure will cover for me. I'll tell Jim I'm going on a little trip with her. But I need to work up to it, make sure I have all the details in order."

"Oh honey, that'll be great. I can't wait to see you."

"I know," Kenzie said, now smiling herself.

She heard footsteps upstairs and was suddenly on alert.

"Sorry, Parker," she whispered. "I hear Jim upstairs. He's up. I have to go."

"Okay, baby," Parker said quickly. "I love you."

"I love you too," Kenzie replied and she quickly disconnected from Skype.

She heard soft footsteps on the stairs and looked up. Jim was there, barefoot, wearing a robe.

"Who were you talking to?" he asked.

"Nobody," Kenzie said, struggling to keep her voice steady. Her heart was pounding.

"I heard you talking."

"Somebody shared a YouTube video on Facebook. I was watching that."

Jim stared at her for a few seconds. Was he trying to determine if she was lying?

"Well," he finally said, "it's after ten. Aren't you coming to bed?"

"Soon," she nodded. "I'll be up in a little while."

Jim glared at her, as if he were weighing the advantages of another argument about syncing their bed times. Finally, he sighed and turned, going back upstairs, shaking his head as if he couldn't figure her out.

Kenzie took a deep breath and slowly let it out, still hearing her pulse thumping in her ears.

Mason Dodd settled into his role as maître d', largely because there was not much expected of him. Wear the Edward Scissorhands suit, greet the customer at the door, and lead him – or sometimes her – to the bedroom where Sonya and Monica were already getting funky, the smell of sex already wafting through the air. That became their *modus operandi* since it very quickly made the customer horny.

It very quickly made Mason horny as well. Opening the door for the customer, he might see Sonya and Monica kissing, fondling each other's breasts, or playing with their sex toys. One time, when the customer had been stuck in a traffic jam and arrived late, Sonya and Monica hadn't waited. They were already busy scissoring when Mason directed the customer into the room. Another time, they were playing with one of their favorite toys, a metallic dildo that they called Tin Lezzie.

After the customer was deposited into their hands, Mason was on his own until the session was over. Often, depending on what he saw when he opened the door, he had to go into his bathroom for a while, for a do-it-yourself session of his own.

But he became accustomed to the routine. Monica had been right. They charged more for the session, and they were having multiple sessions per evening – sometimes as many as three. When that was the case, Mason went to bed. The final customer had to find his own way out, or more often than not, was escorted out by Sonya or Monica.

With the popularity of their venture, Sonya eventually quit her job at Sears. Monica still worked at the sex shop, but only part time. Within a few months, they moved into a house that Sonya found, one with three bedrooms, and a larger room for their 'commercial' activities. While it was meant to be a den or office, the room contained a bed and other assorted equipment. They called it the Rumpus Room.

At that time, Monica officially moved in with them.

Mason woke up with a start, looking around his room, listening. He wasn't sure what he had heard. He had the impression that someone was talking to him, but he couldn't quite focus on the sound.

He got up and went out in the hallway, still listening. He stood outside the Rumpus Room, but it was quiet. The voice came from down the hall. Sometimes, when they weren't entertaining clients, Sonya and Monica made love, sometimes spending the night together in the same bed. But they still kept separate rooms. Outside Monica's room, he heard the voice again.

"Come in, Mason."

He opened the door quietly. He could see a mound in Monica's bed where she was lying. The street light across the street filtered through the curtains, casting a warped trapezoidal shape on the covers, and illuminated the room softly. He couldn't see Monica's face, since the window sill cast a shadow on the upper part of her bed. But then she spoke again.

"Don't just stand there, you moron. Fuck me."

Just the notion aroused Mason. Especially the fact that she would actually be asking for it. They had fondled each other on a few occasions, and Monica even made him cum a couple of times after that first contact. But they had never actually 'done the deed.' His mother seemed to discourage it. Not verbally, but just the way she acted, as if it irritated her.

Mason wasn't sure if it was because of him, or because she was jealous of Monica.

But now, his mother was asleep in her room, and Monica was calling him to her bed. He certainly had no desire to displease her. He closed the door behind him and went to the side of her bed.

He lifted the covers and the street light illuminated her body. She slept in the nude.

Well, of course she did, Mason smiled to himself.

He slipped off his shorts and got in bed with her. He touched her, caressing her breast, feeling her nipple grow hard in his hand.

"Oh yeah, that's nice," she said. "Feel my pussy."

He moved his hand down her side, over her hip and then down, between her legs. He felt the closely cropped fuzz of hair and the mounds of soft skin dipping down into the valley.

"Mmmmm," Monica moaned. She squirmed and opened her legs a little, and the valley spread apart. He rubbed his finger along the ridges, feeling them grow warm and damp, and then he slipped his finger inside. He explored the unfamiliar curves and crevices, and he could hear her breathing intensify.

Leaning on one elbow, and now fully erect, Mason was rubbing against Monica's hip as he inserted a second finger. He inclined his head and took her nipple in his mouth. She moaned softly again and continued squirming for a few moments.

Then, without warning, Monica jerked, and for an instant, Mason thought he had hurt her.

"Mason, what the fuck are you doing?" she asked in an alarmed whisper.

"You called me," Mason replied, feeling suddenly confused.

"Honey, I didn't call you. I was asleep." He felt her hand on his, lingering for just a moment, before she pulled his fingers out of her. "You were dreaming."

Mason was feeling increasingly disoriented.

"Maybe you were talking in your sleep," he suggested.

"I don't know," she said skeptically. "Nobody's ever told me I talk in my sleep." She got out of bed and picked up a t-shirt off a chair, slipping it on. "Come on, babe. Let's get you back to bed."

He got up, now embarrassed by his still erect penis, fully illuminated in the trapezoid of light. He pulled his shorts on and came around the bed, feeling stupid and uncoordinated. Monica put her arm around him and guided him out the door, down the hall, and back to his room.

As he got back in his bed, Monica pulled the covers up.

"Are you sure you didn't call me?" Mason asked again, but with waning certainty.

"I'm sure, honey. It was a dream."

The boy sighed and shook his head on his pillow.

"It sounded so real."

Kenzie," Brad said assuming a stern expression, as he leaned against Kenzie's desk, "what's going on? You seem distracted lately. It's like your mind is a million miles away."

No, only 1,684, she thought.

"I'm fine," she answered, shaking her head. "Why? What's wrong?"

She was wearing a green and rust plaid skirt and a lightweight turtleneck in a shade of green that particularly complimented her fair skin and her luxuriant red hair. It also complimented her figure, and Brad seemed to have to concentrate to keep focused on her eyes.

"Well, for instance, a couple of days ago, I assigned you to oversee the setup for the Sawyer exhibit." He raised his eyebrows, as if expecting Kenzie to respond. She nodded. "I was just looking at the space and it looks as if you've completely disregarded my instructions about the lighting. I don't see a single spotlight in place."

"That's right," Kenzie said. "Mr. Sawyer decided that the spots were too harsh and he said he wanted to go with softer indirect lighting. I mentioned that to you and I made a note in Mr. Sawyer's file."

Brad turned his head slightly to look at her out the corner of his eye, as if he didn't believe her.

"I didn't look in the file, but you didn't tell me about it."

Yes I did, you pompous ass, she thought. When you were busy playing StarCraft on your computer.

"I'm sorry," she replied. "I was sure I told you, but like I said, I did document it in his file."

Brad sighed and lowered his head, making a point to look at the curve of her breasts as he did so. Then he looked back at her face.

"Well, okay, that's one thing," he said. "But in the last week or two, I've also noticed a change in the way you deal with visitors."

"Has somebody complained?" Kenzie asked.

"No, nobody has complained. I'm hoping to rectify the situation before it gets to that point. You just seem distracted lately. Are you not happy here?"

"No, Brad, it's not that. I'm fine, but you're right. I have been kind of distracted."

"Anything I can do to help?" Brad offered, assuming what he probably thought was a sympathetic expression.

"No, just personal things I have to deal with. But thank you."

"Okay. Well, I'm here. If there's anything I can do, just let me know."

Kenzie sighed as she got out of her car. It had been a shitty day. After the scolding in the morning, she had felt Brad watching her all day long. She wasn't sure if he was being especially observant of her work, or if he was just ogling her. Probably both.

Now that she was home, she didn't know if it would be any better. But at least it was Friday, and she would have tomorrow morning to herself, when Jim went to his friend's house to work on the Model T.

She cherished those few hours on Saturday morning, time she had to herself, away from Jim's prying eyes and suspicious comments and critical tone. Occasionally that time stretched into the afternoon. But all good things must come to an end, and it was the same with her Saturdays. They always culminated with bedroom time.

She reached back in the car and got her purse and the bag of groceries she had picked up, and she pushed the button on the garage door remote. As she walked toward the door into the house, she felt close to tears, and she didn't know why.

She stopped, took a deep breath, blew it out, and then continued.

Jim was sitting at the kitchen table when she walked in. He looked up at her.

Shit! Another stern face.

"Hi," Kenzie said, trying to sound cheerful.

"You're late," Jim said, as Kenzie began pulling items out of the grocery bag.

"I called you and told you I was stopping at the store for a few things. And then there was traffic." She also went to the bank to cash Parker's check, but she didn't mention that. Five crisp one hundred dollar bills were folded in half and stuck in her skirt pocket, ready to stash in a safe hiding place, as soon as she found one.

"You wore that to work?" Jim asked.

Kenzie looked down at her clothes, then back at Jim.

"Yes, why?"

"What are you advertising?"

"What? Jim, I'm completely covered. There's no cleavage, my skirt is several inches below my knee and I'm wearing boots. I'm showing almost nothing."

"Yeah, I'll bet Brad loved that skin-tight sweater."

"It's not skin-tight, Jim. It's form-fitting, yes, but not that tight."

"Kenzie, are you having an affair?" Jim asked abruptly.

145

She stopped what she was doing and looked at him. Her face reflected the surprise and shock that she felt about him even suggesting such a thing. She also felt guilt and panic, attached to the picture of Parker in her mind, and she hoped that *didn't* show on her face.

"Why would you ask that?"

"You just don't seem to care about me anymore. You're apparently not interested in having a baby with me. You make me go to bed alone every fucking night!"

"Honey," she replied, trying to keep her voice even, "we've talked about that. Our schedules are different. You get up a lot earlier than I do, so you go to bed earlier. That's all."

He waited a moment, then he raised an eyebrow.

"That's it? Out of the three things I mentioned, that's the only one you respond to?"

"Jim," she sighed, "of course I care about you. And we've talked about having a baby, but we still haven't settled on anything. I told you that last week when you got mad at me about the birth control pills."

"Kenzie, nowadays, you're in a shitty mood all the time," he continued. "Just about the only time I ever see you smile anymore is when you're on Facebook. And incidentally, I've also noticed lately that you started logging out of Facebook on your phone. You used to just close the app."

"How would you know that? Are you checking my phone?"

"You don't even smile when we're making love," he continued, ignoring her question. "The last several times we had sex, you couldn't cum. I used to make you cum all the time. I'm not doing anything different now.

"So I'll ask you again: Are you having an affair?"

"Jim, when would I have time to have an affair? I work a full time job. I'm with you the rest of the time."

"Yeah, except Saturdays."

She felt a brief moment of panic at the thought of possibly having her Saturday time taken away from her.

"Well, I think it's important that we have some time to ourselves, don't you?" she asked quietly.

"Yeah, and you still haven't answered my question."

"I'm not having an affair on Saturdays!" she replied exasperated.

"You got a lot of nerve getting mad at me," Jim said, picking up on her tone. He stood up and faced her directly, that vein in his forehead standing out. "I'm the one with complaints here, and you think you have the right to get mad at me?"

"I'm sorry, Jim," Kenzie said. "I didn't mean to sound angry. I'm not."

She leaned one hand on the counter, trying to calm her breathing. She felt her heart pounding, her pulse throbbing in her ears, and she was aware of the dots of perspiration popping out on her forehead.

Jim looked at her for a moment longer, then he nodded.

"Okay, so I guess it's time we make some decisions. One, you'll go to bed when I go to bed. No more staying up late at night chatting with your little Facebook friends."

Kenzie looked up at him.

"Jim, no." It didn't come out nearly as forcefully as she had hoped.

"Two, as of now, you will stop taking your birth control pills and we're going to start trying to have a baby."

Kenzie was starting to feel even more despondent than usual. She could feel a lump forming in her throat and tears welling up in her eyes.

"Three, you will do whatever you need to do to stop being such a fucking downer." He punctuated this by knocking on the table. "Damn, woman! You're nothing but a pain in the ass anymore."

Apparently sick of looking at her, he stormed out of the kitchen and up the stairs.

Kenzie slowly turned back to the groceries on the counter. But they had to wait. She couldn't do anything with them.

She couldn't see them through the tears in her eyes.

Hunter jerked awake when the glass in his hand tipped and spilled on his thigh. Adding insult to injury, Jarvis, who had been sleeping curled up on Hunter's lap, was startled by the sudden movement, jabbing his claws into Hunter's leg, and darted away with a hiss.

"Shit!" Hunter said as he quickly set his glass down on the coffee table and attempted to brush the bourbon off his leg, rolling up little clinging mats of damp cat hair with it. He picked up pages from Katherine's file, which had fluttered down onto the floor, and placed them back on the open file folder beside him on the love seat.

Hunter made it a practice to examine Kathy's report and his hand-written notes on Jenny Norbert every evening, just hoping that on a different day, after different experiences, and contact with different people, something might present itself in a different light. Something that had seemed unimportant or irrelevant might suddenly make sense.

Once again, he was disappointed.

Two crime scenes three years apart, with the exact same M.O., but with absolutely nothing linking them to each other. Neither Hunter nor Kathy knew the Norberts. They lived in different parts of town, ran in different social circles. Their lives didn't seem to overlap in any area that Hunter was able to isolate.

Kathy and Jenny Norbert were different as well. Kathy was twenty-five when she was killed, Jenny Norbert was thirty-eight.

Kathy was tanned and auburn-haired, Jenny Norbert was fair-skinned and blonde. Kathy had green eyes, Jenny Norbert's eyes were blue. Their body types, their clothing, their cars, everything was different.

Even the locations and times of the killings. Kathy was kidnapped in broad daylight and taken to a strange house where she was killed. Jenny Norbert was killed in her own home late at night.

And not a trace of physical evidence left at either crime scene.

Hunter had always heard there's no such thing as a perfect crime, and yet here, apparently, were two of them.

As he compared the information on the killings, he slowly scratched the scars on his wrists. He just couldn't seem to ease the irritation. Maybe Dr. Jeffries' concerns had been valid. Maybe Hunter really wasn't up for this. The resolution of Kathy's murder was eluding him, and now, here was another one, equally confounding.

The discouragement was piling up, like a wall being erected around him. Each day that went by without a single clue being added to either file felt like one more brick being placed in the wall of the room that was beginning to enclose him. He'd been in that room before, and he didn't like it. It was dark, cold, hopeless.

Back then, cutting his wrists had seemed like the only way out of that room. And he had almost made it. But then Parker just happened to drop by. Hunter's escape turned into a few weeks in the psych ward and a new project for Dr. Jeffries.

There were times when he still regretted not making his own exit.

It didn't help that the last time he and Kathy saw each other, they had been angry. That stupid fight they had on Monday morning, Labor Day, when he had to go to work. There was a virus going around and they were short-handed.

Why did he get angry at her? She just wanted to spend time with him. What the hell was wrong with that? Of course, he didn't think that would be the last time he saw her alive. Nobody ever thinks that way. We get so caught up in our stupid little irritations, and the next thing you know, it's too late to take back what was said.

That's a lot of what had sent him into that dark, cold room. Losing her, obviously, was bad. But losing her with that stupid fight being her last memory of him was a massive weight.

Hunter sighed heavily and sat back, shaking his head and chafing both wrists on his pant legs. He couldn't let that darkness take him again. He had to stay focused. He owed that to Kathy. And to Lily.

He closed the file folder and got up. It was late. He'd get some sleep and start again in the morning. He also had another case he needed to take care of tomorrow. The kind he didn't like, but it helped pay the bills.

He despised the cheating spouse cases, following and photographing a suspected adulterer. But he needed income if he was going to keep working on Kathy's and Jenny Norbert's cases. He felt slimy taking those cases, but they were usually quick and easy.

He took his glass into the kitchen, poured the diluted bourbon that was left into the sink, and put the glass in the dishwasher. He put the folder down on the counter, in front of Kathy's picture. The folder was closed, but every detail was still burned into his brain. He never stopped thinking about it.

Three years was a long time between serial killings. Could this be a copycat? That could explain how, despite the similarity of the method of killing, there were no similarities in the details about the victims.

He turned out the light and went into the bathroom. He took his toothbrush out of the glass holder Kathy had bought. The one with their initials etched in the side. It was only about a year ago that he had finally gotten rid of her toothbrush.

He started brushing his teeth, remembering how they had sometimes jockeyed for space in front of the sink. Standing shoulder to shoulder, pushing against each other. The outcome was never a foregone conclusion. Kathy had been considerably smaller than Hunter, but she often braced her foot against the baseboard, getting some pretty good leverage when she pushed.

Hunter rinsed his mouth and turned out the light.

He went into the bedroom and, as he got undressed, he looked at the picture on the dresser. Hunter and Kathy on their honeymoon in Puerto Vallarta. They were both smiling, carefree. It was a sun-soaked week, and the photograph showed a sample of it. The sunlight cast an almost blinding glare off of Kathy's shiny auburn hair.

Hunter cocked his head to the side as something suddenly occurred to him. Jenny Norbert had blonde hair and blue eyes, just like Lily. Hunter knew he was grasping at straws, but with nothing to go on, he'd grasp at every straw he could get his hands on.

Could Lily have been the intended target, and Kathy just happened to be with her? It was an intriguing possibility, though it didn't explain why the killer carried out his ritual on Kathy first, giving Lily time and opportunity to get away. He had to admit that hair and eye color seemed like a pretty flimsy thing to build a murder career on, but serial killings had been carried out based on less than that.

He looked at his watch. It was almost midnight. This wasn't a break. It wasn't new evidence, nothing important enough to wake R.J. about. Hunter decided he'd wait and call him tomorrow. They hadn't spoken and compared notes in a while, anyway. They were due.

Maybe he'd also go see Parker and Lily tomorrow too, see if he could make any connection between them and the Norberts.

He didn't have much confidence in that. Parker's circles were not that different from his own. But he had to check. Just in case Lily's blue eyes and blonde hair were the key.

He thought about Lily, and how brave she'd been these last few days, willing to retrace her steps on that horrible day. Reliving her last moments with Kathy, trying to dredge up every awful detail she can remember.

That little girl's quite a trooper, he thought with a smile.

O h, shit," Arden said. He had heard a car pull up into the driveway and had gone to the front window to see who it was.

"What's the matter?" JuleighAnn asked.

"Kenzie's here," he replied, watching as she approached the front door. He turned to look at JuleighAnn. "Her eyes are almost as red as her hair."

JuleighAnn got up from the sofa and opened the door just as Kenzie rang the bell.

"Come in, honey," she said. "What's wrong?"

Kenzie started crying anew, and JuleighAnn put her arms around her, as Molson came bounding up at the sound of the door, his nails clicking on the hardwood floor. Arden grabbed the dog's collar and looked at JuleighAnn.

Do you want me to go? he silently mouthed toward her. She nodded over Kenzie's shoulder, and he grabbed his jacket and Molson's leash from hooks on the wall beside the door. Fastening the leash to the excited Golden Retriever's collar, Arden slipped his free arm into his jacket, leaving it hanging as he reached for the door handle. He tried to get Molson past the two women without causing too much disruption.

He wasn't successful.

Molson was anxious to see Kenzie, but then, when he noticed the front door was open and his leash was on, he made a sudden dash out the doorway, spinning Arden around to follow. Still struggling to get his jacket on, and to regain his balance, Arden ran out the door behind him.

JuleighAnn closed the door and guided Kenzie toward the family room at the back of the house, overlooking the lake. After getting her settled on the sofa with a cup of coffee, and refreshing her own, JuleighAnn sat next to her. She pushed a box of tissues closer to her.

"Jim?" she asked. Kenzie nodded.

"He's made some decisions," she said, blotting her nose. "Among them, I am to go to bed when he does, at eight o'clock, because he doesn't like going to bed alone. And we are going to start working on having a baby."

JuleighAnn looked at her with pursed lips and raised eyebrows. The look transmitted sympathy, but also something else. JuleighAnn usually tried to avoid the classic clichéd line, "and how does that make you feel?" But this look, she found, often had the same effect.

"I guess that first one is not really that big a deal," Kenzie said. "I kind of feel like a child whining about my bed time."

As a therapist, JuleighAnn generally avoided volunteering her opinion. But as a friend, she was sometimes more willing.

"Understandable," she said, "since he's *treating* you like a child." Kenzie sniffed and nodded her head.

"True. I don't like being forced to do things. I don't like being told how to dress. I don't like being given a small allowance for necessities. I don't like being told when to go to bed."

"But you're not here because of your bed time, are you?"

"No," Kenzie said quietly as she reached for another tissue. "The baby is the big one. I *want* to have a baby. I really do." Another tear rolled down her cheek before she could catch it. "But I know I don't want one with Jim."

JuleighAnn nodded.

"Have you decided what you're going to do?"

156

Kenzie sat motionless for a while, looking downward, studying her fingers, warped by the refraction of her tears. Then she took a deep breath and looked up at JuleighAnn.

"I'm going to work up my courage and talk to him," she announced slowly and firmly, "and tell him that I'm not ready, and we'll just have to wait a bit longer."

"That was easy," JuleighAnn commented with a smile. "I've hardly said a thing."

"I feel stronger when I'm with you," Kenzie said, blotting her eyes. "I'll probably turn spineless again when I'm with him. I don't suppose you'd tell him?"

She smiled to show that she was only kidding. JuleighAnn returned the smile.

"And in the meantime," Kenzie continued, "I'm going to book a flight out to North Carolina, just to meet Parker and see what he's really like."

"Hmm," JuleighAnn said, nodding. "Well, that's an improvement, at least. Just be careful. Even though you're still officially in your relationship with Jim, Parker could be considered a rebound."

"I never understood what's so wrong with that," Kenzie said. "What's the problem with finding some happiness after a bad relationship?"

"Not a thing," JuleighAnn replied. "But it's important to look for it with a clear head, not a broken heart. Fresh out of a bad relationship, and especially while you're still in one, there's the danger of falling victim to the 'grass is always greener' syndrome."

"But what if the grass really *is* greener?"

"It's wonderful if it is. But a person likely won't know for certain while they've got their blinders on. They see Mr. Rebound and he's perfect. He doesn't do the things that drive them crazy about their last relationship. But at the same time, his shining armor covers up the things he *does* do that might drive them equally crazy.

"Now I'm not saying that Parker *does* do anything that will drive you crazy. It's entirely possible that he's Mr. Right. I'm just saying be careful."

Kenzie nodded.

"Thank you," she said.

"You're welcome. You're such a sweet girl. I want nothing but the best for you." Kenzie started tearing up again. "And I want you to know," JuleighAnn continued, "that whatever happens, I've got your back. I care about you and your happiness, and I'll be behind you on whatever you ultimately decide. And if I can help with anything, just let me know."

"Well," Kenzie said, "now that you mention it, I could use an alibi."

JuleighAnn gave her a confused frown.

"I need a reason to give to Jim about why I'm going to North Carolina. I want to use you as my cover story. I thought I'd tell him that I was accompanying you out there for a few days, since he'd never let me take a trip like that alone."

"I don't know, Kenzie," JuleighAnn said hesitantly. "You want me to lie to Jim for you?"

"No, that's on me. I basically just want to use your name. He knows we're good friends, but he hardly knows you at all. Chances are he won't ever call you. In fact, I'd be surprised if he even knows how to contact you."

JuleighAnn sat back and sighed. It was against her better judgment, but . . . .

"Okay," she conceded. "I did say I've got your back."

Kenzie sprang forward and wrapped JuleighAnn in a warm, affectionate hug.

"Oh, thank you so much, Jules." JuleighAnn hugged her back, then looked at her.

158

"Well, don't thank me yet," JuleighAnn said. "Just hope Jim doesn't call me. I suck at lying. That's more Arden's department."

Club Carolina was attached to a sprawling Marriott Hotel in north Raleigh. It was also apparently a popular lunch site. The restaurant was crowded when Parker arrived, but fortunately Marlys had reserved a table and was already seated.

The hostess led Parker toward the table, and Marlys stood up to greet him when she saw him approaching. Instead of a pant suit, as she had worn the other times he had seen her, today she was wearing wedge sandals and a skirt and blouse. The skirt showed her shapely legs from a couple of inches above the knee, and the button-front blouse was open about three buttons down, showing some cleavage.

Parker thought both looked great.

"Damn, girl," he said shaking her hand, as he looked her up and down. He smiled and showed dimples so deep that people often thought they must rub against his teeth. For a moment, he forgot she was twenty years older than him, especially when she grinned like a teenager at the compliment.

As they sat down, the waitress approached their table, and Parker saw that Marlys already had a glass of white wine in front of her.

"I got here about a half hour ago," she explained.

"Jim Beam on the rocks," he said to the waitress, who then smiled and left.

Parker looked at Marlys. He had known she was attractive. Today, she looked downright pretty. Her makeup was less businesslike and more fun. Her short salt and pepper hair, rather than being brushed back, was kind of wispy around her face.

"So watcha been up to, son?" she asked.

Parker shook his head and smiled at her, flashing his dimples again.

"Just keeping busy working, ma'am."

For just a moment, Parker thought she winced at something painful.

"Well, that's good you're keeping busy. But could I ask a small favor of you? Don't call me ma'am."

"Tell you what," Parker said, "you stop calling me son, I'll stop calling you ma'am."

"Deal," she said, and they both giggled. That surprised Parker who had never been much of a giggler.

They spent a few minutes perusing the menu. When the waitress returned and set his drink down in front of him, they decided to order their meals. A garden salad with crab and avocado for Marlys, and the pot roast with potatoes and carrots for Parker.

"So," Parker said, "I hear you might have some more modeling work for me?"

"Oh," Marlys exclaimed, "hon, I have been fielding calls for the past couple of weeks, from ad agencies, modeling agencies, talent scouts. People have seen your pictures in that calendar and they all want to know, 'Who is that young god?'"

Parker looked down and swirled his drink, blushing a little. Marlys leaned forward and placed her hand on his wrist.

"Hon," she said, "I think it's so adorable that you blush about that. You aren't spoiled by the stuck-up attitude of a lot of the models I've worked with."

Parker noticed that she kept her hand on his wrist. Besides the embarrassment, he was also feeling a little nervous. He made it a point to take a drink, moving his wrist from under Marlys' hand. If she noticed, she gave no indication, and they talked about some of the modeling jobs that were proposed, until the food arrived.

"So, Parker, what do you think about being a professional model? Had you ever thought about it before?"

"No ma'- Marlys. Not until you approached me at The Sawmill." He paused and thought for a moment. "I do like building houses, but it's hard work. Hot and miserable in the summertime, cold and miserable in the winter, if I can even get jobs then. And I don't get near as much money for it as I'd like. But a thousand bucks for a couple hours of standing around in that tool belt, I gotta admit, that was pretty cool."

Marlys smiled, remembering his body as it had looked that day. He was wearing a long sleeved shirt now, and though the cuffs were rolled up a couple of times, for the most part, it only showed a hint of his torso.

But she remembered his wide, smooth chest, and the sexy tattoos lacing across the left side of it. She remembered the tiny shorts that she had arranged to be his wardrobe. She remembered the top of his pubic hair showing above the open waistband. She remembered that the waistband was so low and the legs so high that it necessitated him positioning his genitals to the side, causing the bulges to stand out even more against the front of his hip.

"Yes, well I can't promise keeping you busy all the time with jobs like that," she said as she unbuttoned one more button in response to the heat she suddenly felt, and she tried to inconspicuously flap the front of her blouse a little, to cool herself off. "But I think I *can* keep a good supply of supplemental income coming your way."

"That sounds good, Marlys. Let's do it!"

She grinned as a double entendre flashed through her mind.

"You know," she said slowly, lowering her voice a little, "I don't know how you feel about this, but one of the companies that called about you is in the adult entertainment industry."

Parker looked at her and, for a moment, stopped chewing the bite of pot roast he had just put in his mouth. Then he finished chewing and swallowed before speaking.

"What? You mean pornography?"

"Well, not really," Marlys said, trying to choose her words carefully. "It's not so much what you'd see in Hustler magazine. It's more like what you might see late at night on Cinemax."

She looked at his face, watching his reaction. She smiled slightly as she saw that he was thinking about it, instead of just immediately rejecting the idea. She reached out and closed her hand over his in what she hoped seemed like a protective gesture.

"Honey," she said, "you can turn down anything you're not comfortable with, but I can tell you for sure these jobs pay decent money."

In the back of Parker's mind, he had been thinking about how much a divorce might cost him. Getting free of Lily would surely not come cheap. He hadn't done any research on it yet, but he was pretty sure that the cost of Lily's mental health treatment would very likely come into play in determining alimony.

But sex films? Or sexy layouts for magazines? He wasn't sure if he was ready to go that route.

On the other hand, he had seen bits and pieces of the Cinemax movies she had mentioned. It's not like they're X-rated films. A lot of movement, but nothing really explicit.

"How about we put that aside for now," Parker said, "and we just think about some of those other jobs."

"Fair enough," Marlys replied with a nod and a pat on his hand. "We'll just put that on the back burner for now."

But that back burner sure was turned up high! The thought of being naked in front of other people, acting like he was having sex, stayed in the front of his mind. He thought about it every time Marlys touched him, every time he saw her lick her lips, every time he looked over at her and saw the top of her breasts in her flimsy bra. Every time she said something flirtatious, or looked at him lustfully. Which she seemed to be doing more frequently.

Damn, she was a sexy woman!

The pounding in his ears was distracting. He tried to focus on what she was saying.

"It's a beautiful afternoon. There's a nice little park out there. Maybe we could just go for a walk while we talk about some of the jobs you *are* interested in."

"I don't know, Marlys. I'm thinking I should get home to my wife."

"Hmm, yeah I saw that ring on your finger, but I wasn't sure how much it meant."

Parker looked down at the ring and self-consciously twisted it on his finger. How much *did* it mean to him? He had already decided that he didn't love Lily anymore. He was already being at least mentally and emotionally unfaithful to her with Kenzie, even though they had never actually been together.

"That's quite a case of apprehension you got there," Marlys said in response to his hesitation.

Parker looked back up at Marlys, wondering how she could so quickly see what he had been struggling with for so long. The ring didn't mean shit. Not anymore. He and Lily were done. He just hadn't figured out how to tell her yet.

Marlys finished her salad and purposefully wiped her lips with her napkin. Then she pushed her chair back a little. Sitting there in that relaxed pose, her blouse still unbuttoned a little lower, Parker could see even more of the top of her breasts.

As she got out a compact and replaced the lipstick on her lips, she crossed her legs. And they were damn nice legs! Sitting down, her skirt came to about the middle of her thigh, and those thighs kept tugging at Parker's eyes, especially when she started swinging her foot back and forth a little.

One of the times he glanced at them, he looked up at her and saw her looking back at him, and she smiled. Parker quickly looked away again.

Thing is, he thought, it may be over with Lily, but it was just starting with Kenzie. In self-defense, to combat the pull of Marlys' legs on his attention, he made a point of trying to remember if he had seen any pictures on Facebook of Kenzie's legs. He was flipping through her pictures in his mind. He saw her flaming red hair, her warm brown eyes, her porcelain skin. But he couldn't remember seeing any pictures of her legs.

As he was trying to concentrate on Kenzie's pictures, and on the last couple of carrots on his plate, Marlys idly scratched her thigh. Once again, she caught him looking.

And again, she smiled at him. It wasn't a scary seductress smile. Just a sweet, friendly, really pretty smile. And Parker smiled back at her.

"You know, sugar," she said softly, just above a whisper, "I can see myself falling head over heels in bed with you."

And suddenly, he dropped that mental file folder of Kenzie's pictures, and every damn one of them landed face down on the floor of his brain.

chizophrenia was such a strange and ugly word. But it was a word that had been applied to Mason for about a year now. After that first time in Monica's bed, he kept hearing the voices. Sometimes it was Monica's voice, other times they were strange messages in voices he didn't recognize.

So the doctor introduced him to another strange and ugly word.

Antipsychotic. Ugly because of the implication. That without the drugs, Mason would be psychotic.

Ugly, also, because of the side effects. Dizziness, headaches, diarrhea. And he was always so damn tired. This was definitely a case of the cure being worse than the disease.

Mason was lying on the sofa with the TV on, but barely paying attention to it. The front door opened and Monica appeared, much like she had four years before, when Mason first met her. She was fanning herself with one hand and had a bundle of something in the other. Her glossy obsidian hair was longer, and her tight skirt considerably shorter.

The sex shop was much more lax on their dress code than JC Penney had been.

"Hi, Mace," she said in that sexy, sandpapery voice.

He nodded and smiled as he looked her up and down. At seventeen, he still looked a little older than he was. And he was still in love with Monica.

Mason was sure she loved him in return. She had never said it, but she was always tender with him, caring. She still touched him often, and not just to tease him as she had early on. There was something else there.

The first time he entered her, he could see it in her sky blue eyes. And every time since.

But she didn't advertise it. She was torn. She was in love with Sonya, too.

"Hi babe," Sonya said as she came into the living room. "I thought I heard you come in." She gave Monica a quick kiss, then looked at the bundle she was holding. "What's this?"

Monica's face brightened up and she led Sonya toward the love seat. She put the package down on the coffee table and turned to Sonya.

"You know what we've been talking about for so long?" she said. "Well, I decided, let's stop talking about it and give it a try."

Sonya's eyes blazed with excitement as she looked at the package.

"Are you sure?" she asked as she looked back at Monica. "You don't think it's too freaky? I mean I know you've been curious about it too, but I was the one who was always more interested."

"Absolutely!" Monica said quietly, leaning against Sonya's shoulder. "What could be more sexy?" She glanced at Mason and her smile faded just a fraction.

Mason turned the light out and got in bed, turning his bedside lamp on. He picked up the book he was reading and opened it. He always went to bed early now. Even after he stopped taking his medication. He had to keep up appearances.

He'd rather hear the voices, see the hallucinations, than to have to experience the feeling of being sick all the time. He knew

168

he could be smart about it. Keep up the schedule of going to bed early. Feign a dizzy spell every once in a while. Even occasionally go into the bathroom for extended times.

Visions and memories of Monica in little or no attire gave him something to do in there. Something much more pleasant than diarrhea!

Sometime around ten o'clock, Mason opened his eyes. His book was on his chest. He must have dozed off. He listened, unsure of what had woken him.

He heard a distant rustling sound and a voice, but he couldn't tell what was being said.

He shook his head. Being aware of one's condition definitely had its advantages. Knowing he was subject to hallucinations, he could reject them. Refuse to react.

He picked up his book and looked at it, trying to decide if he wanted to read some more or go to sleep.

"No! No!" he heard. And more rustling. That part was new. He had never heard sound effects before.

And this time, the voice sounded like Sonya's.

Mason got up and opened his door. The sound was louder. Frantic sobbing, rustling sounds, and again, the frenzied "No! No! No!"

He walked slowly down the hallway, listening. He needed to be sure what he was hearing was real, before he embarrassed himself. He stopped outside the Rumpus Room. The sounds were coming from in there.

He didn't want to give away that he was hearing things again, so he quietly opened the door just a crack and peeked in. He couldn't see Sonya or Monica, but there was plastic spread out on the floor. And Sonya's voice was a little louder now.

Mason opened the door wider. He stood there looking into the room for a few seconds, trying to determine if what he was seeing was real or a hallucination.

169

Sonya was kneeling on the floor, wearing a bright henna colored wig and a harness teddy made of a few criss-crossing leather straps, held together with buckles and metal rings, but which covered almost nothing. She was frantically scrambling around in a spreading pool of blood.

Monica, in a bright yellow wig and a similar teddy, was lying on her back in the blood.

She wasn't moving.

Mason saw a hinged wooden box opened on the floor near Monica's shoulder, about the size of the package she had brought home, and in it were an assortment of knives and scalpels fitted into a molded interior. A scalpel was on the floor a couple of feet away from where Sonya was still whimpering and sobbing, shuffling around Monica, pressing on her arm.

The inside of Monica's right upper arm, and down her right side, were dark with blood. Her arm, her chest and her face were covered with bloody smudges.

Sonya's hands were similarly smeared with blood, as were her legs and her face. Tears left light streaks through the blood on her face, as she pulled a blood-soaked rag from Monica's arm and desperately reached for another. As she did so, she looked up and saw Mason.

"Mace! Call 911!"

Mason watched through squinted eyes, frowning, certain that this was just a horrible hallucination. It had to be. But then Sonya screamed at him, then sat back wailing, looking down at Monica.

Mason came slowly into the room, his bare feet slipping on the bloody plastic.

"We were experimenting with blood play," Sonya sobbed. "We just wanted to try something new, with just the two of us."

As Mason approached, an expression of dread and horror slowly spread across his face as he gradually accepted the reality of the scene.

170

"Monica didn't want it to show," she continued, whimpering between every two or three words, "and she suggested her inner arm."

Mason was now standing between them, looking down at Monica. Her eyes were open a little, but not moving, only a crescent of pale blue showing beneath the dilated irises. She wasn't breathing.

"I guess she wasn't expecting the prick of the blade and she jerked her arm. But my knee was right there and her arm bounced back." Sonya started crying harder again, as Mason looked down at Monica's inner arm. The puncture was small, insignificant. But some part of his brain remembered a science class, human anatomy, and he recognized the approximate location of the brachial artery.

"Mason, it was only a couple of minutes ago!" she asserted, her tears washing twin tracks through the blood on her cheeks.

He knew that was all it took. The major arteries carried a person's entire blood volume through their body in one to three minutes, depending on their heart rate. If an artery was cut, the person could bleed out in as little as a minute.

Mason knelt beside Monica, his knees momentarily slipping in the blood, looking at her face through the distortion of the tears welling up in his eyes. He reached out and gently touched her face, already cool under his fingers, and his tears fell, splashing in the blood caked on her side.

As he looked at her, he remembered times they had spent together, talking, joking around, making love, and he realized that he would never feel her love again. The object of his desire for the last four years was dead.

At his mother's hand.

He remembered Sonya's looks of disapproval when Monica showed him any attention. He remembered Sonya's lack of interest, her sometimes disheartening remarks, going back to the first time he heard her refer to him as her stupid kid, back in the Bronx. He remembered the times she had him lean over the dining room table as she paddled him for some stupid offense, real or imagined.

Mason looked at Sonya, sitting back on her heels, wearing that silly wig of fake orange-brown hair and that ridiculous arrangement of straps, her bare breasts jiggling as she sobbed and muttered unintelligibly. She looked back at him, crying hysterically, her face a bizarre patchwork of emotional pain and sorrow, and blood-smeared horror.

She didn't even seem to notice when he chose a knife with a six-inch curved blade from the box, and in one swift arc of his arm, slashed the blade through her throat, now adding her own blood to the puddles on the floor. Her crying stopped immediately, replaced by a gurgling hiss, the remorse in her eyes quickly changing to shock and surprise, before she fell over on her side.

Hunter drove back toward home from east Durham. He felt dirty, like one of the slimy, low-life detectives he used to make fun of.

But at least he'd be able to keep his utilities turned on for another month.

His cheating spouse job had paid off. Having followed the husband of his client to a cheap motel, Hunter got photographs of him meeting a pretty brunette for a Saturday morning tryst. He even got a good shot of the guilty look on his face as they left the room together a couple of hours later.

While waiting in his car, Hunter had used the time in between to call R.J., to run his theory past him.

"Listen, R.J., I had a thought last night. I admit it's really flimsy, and it doesn't even necessarily get us any closer to catching the guy. But what if Lily was his target and Kathy just happened to be in the wrong place at the wrong time?"

"Doesn't make sense," R.J. replied without hesitation. "Why would he waste time performing a ritualistic murder on somebody who was only secondary to his plan?"

"Yeah, I know. I thought of that too, and I don't have an answer. But I'm just racking my brain trying to find anything that might connect those two murders."

"I don't get it. How would that link them?"

"Because Lily has blonde hair. I know, I already said it was flimsy."

"Okay, I still don't get it," R.J. said. "Jenny Norbert wasn't a blonde."

"Sure she was," Hunter protested, opening one of the folders on the seat beside him. He looked at the photograph he had of Jenny Norbert, posing with her husband. "I'm looking at a picture of her right now."

"Uh, Hunter, where did you get a picture of her?"

"I . . . lifted it from the Norberts' house that morning," Hunter admitted hesitantly.

"Damn it, Hunter! I'm already putting my neck out just sharing my investigation with you. You trying to get me fired?"

"Come on, R.J., I knew Norbert would give me one for the investigation, but he was so eaten up with grief that I didn't want to bother him with it."

"Hunter, you of all people know we got a procedure we're supposed to follow. And I'm already bending it to include you in this."

"My wife was brutally murdered, R.J. You really expect me to give a shit about departmental procedure?"

"No, I don't," R.J. replied angrily, "but if you expect my help and cooperation, you damn well better follow it, anyway."

"Okay," Hunter conceded, "you're right R.J. I'm sorry."

R.J. sighed, followed by a long silence.

"R.J., what are you thinking?"

"I'm thinking I ought to shoot you, you dumb asshole."

"Besides that."

Another extended pause ensued.

"Jenny Norbert wasn't blonde," R.J. finally replied. "You stole an old photo. She dyed her hair a couple of weeks before. Women do that all the time, you know."

"That could be an important point," Hunter said, irritated. "And you didn't see any need to share that information with me?"

"It never occurred to me. I figured you would have seen her hair for yourself when you were there, contaminating the crime scene."

"No," Hunter sighed. "Jenny Norbert had already been carried out in a body bag by the time I got there." Hunter rubbed his eyes. "So what color was her hair?"

"Kind of a reddish brown. Auburn, they're calling it in the report."

Hunter's eyes snapped open.

"Well that's it! Hair color may be the key. I was right. Just not about Lily. Kathy *was* the target. He may have chosen them based on their hair color."

"Could be," R.J. assented. "I figured that might be a possibility from the beginning. But how does that help us catch him?"

"I don't know. It might not. Like I said, it's flimsy. But it's something."

There was another long pause as they both reflected on just how miniscule that link really was.

"I don't suppose you've been able to find anything about a mid-70s Dodge Dart?" Hunter finally asked.

"Without a plate or a VIN? Sorry, no such luck."

"Shit!"

As he neared home, he replayed the conversation in his head. It wasn't sounding any better. After three years on Kathy's case, and over a month on Jenny Norbert's, similar hair color wasn't much to show for their investigations.

He didn't notice that he was fiercely scratching his wrists.

Parker sat back against the pillows, the sheet pulled up over his waist. Marlys was snuggled up against him, under his right arm, her head on his chest. He was absently stroking her upper arm, while she more purposefully caressed his thigh under the sheet. Occasionally, whether by accident or by design, her hand brushed across his penis, now more relaxed than it was a little earlier.

Parker was only semi-conscious of the contact. He was deep in thought. He was amazed at how quickly and unexpectedly this had happened. One minute, he was down in the restaurant, trying desperately not to lust after her body, the next they were up here, in the room that she, somehow, already had.

He was also amazed at how attracted he was to a woman who was old enough to be his mother. But damn! She sure didn't look like his mother!

Once they were in the room and Marlys started undressing, Parker was so distracted by her body, that by the time she was naked, she turned and saw that he was still standing there fully clothed.

For a moment, they both stood there regarding each other. Parker gazed at her body, trim and brown, again not at all what he expected. Her breasts were not large, but they were round and firm, the nipples erect.

"One of us seems to be seriously overdressed," she said. Her tone was joking, but her expression was warm and affectionate as she saw the appreciation on his face. She smiled and decided to lend a hand.

She sidled up to him and unbuttoned his shirt, pushing it back over his considerable shoulders. She softly rubbed his chest, on the tattoo, and traced the path of one of the lines to his nipple. Then she looked up at him and smiled.

Parker remembered when Lily used to do that, and in almost a reflexive movement, he threw his arms around Marlys and crushed his lips against hers. Holding her naked body, tasting her lips and her tongue, he realized how badly he wanted her, the desire bringing tears to his eyes. With Marlys' arms around his neck, Parker grasped both soft cheeks of her ass and pulled her tight against him. When one of the tears splashed on her shoulder, she pulled away and looked up at him.

"Well bless your heart, sugar," she said softly, visibly moved by his emotion.

She looked into his eyes for a moment longer, then reached down and started unfastening his jeans. She tugged them down, then his shorts, revealing that he was already fully erect. She tentatively touched him, looking back into his eyes, watching his reaction as she started to gently stroke his erection. His breath caught in his throat for a moment as she gripped it and used it as a handle to playfully pull him toward the bed, still gazing intently into his eyes.

Then he tripped on the jeans gathered around his ankles.

That initial tension eased a little as they both laughed, and Parker sat down on the side of the bed to take the rest of his clothes off.

He stopped and looked up at her.

"I don't have a condom," he said. Marlys looked at him for a moment.

"I had a hysterectomy years ago, but . . ." Her voice trailed off as she thought. Then she looked back at Parker, and the innocent little boy look on his face. "Well," she smiled at him, "you don't exactly strike me as the type who goes fucking around with anything that moves. I think we'll be okay."

Parker pulled off his shoes and socks, and tossed his jeans and underwear against the wall. Before he could get back up to pull the covers down, Marlys knelt down between his legs. During the interruption, Parker had started going flaccid again, but Marlys brought that initial tension back in an instant as she took him into her mouth, cupping his balls in her hand, gently caressing them.

Oh God! He had almost forgotten how good that felt. Her lips, her tongue, the warm, silky wetness of it. After such a long abstinence, he knew it wouldn't take long.

But then she had stopped. She stood up and directed him to get up as well. She pulled the covers down, lying down on the cool sheets.

Parker looked down at her as she turned toward him, her legs apart just enough for him to see that she was already wet and glistening. She spread her legs apart, making room for him, and he approached her from the foot of the bed. Her musky female smell was so incredibly enticing and drew him in, and he tasted her, hesitantly at first, until she grabbed his head with both hands and pressed his mouth against her.

Using his lips and his tongue against her clit, and a couple of fingers inside her, Marlys was moaning and writhing in a matter of minutes. Suddenly, she let go of his head and lifted hers up to look down at him.

"I want you inside me," she said breathlessly.

Parker didn't need to be asked twice. He rose and moved up so they were face to face, and he slipped his left arm under her neck, while using his right hand to guide his penis inside her. Once he slipped all the way in, feeling her squeeze around him, they both moaned in harmony.

He began moving rhythmically as Marlys wrapped her legs around him, pulling him in. Earlier, he had been right: it wouldn't take long.

He started pumping faster, gritting his teeth, as Marlys pushed her head back, deeper into the pillow, her mouth open and panting. Parker looked at her neck, her shoulders, her breasts bouncing up and down with each thrust. As he heaved into her faster and harder, he felt Marlys' hands gripping his waist, until he finally achieved critical mass.

Parker continued thrusting, pumping into her, filling her, and a few seconds later, Marlys uttered a deep, sustained groan, as if she had been holding her breath and finally let it out.

That had been the good part.

Now, as Parker lay there afterwards, he could feel the guilt creeping in.

Even though he knew it was over with Lily, he felt guilty about the fact that he had actually, physically betrayed her.

And he felt guilty toward Kenzie, too. Their lovemaking had only been verbal, but it had been real. He had felt it, and he knew that she had too.

Had he spoiled everything now?

As Sonya and Monica lay dead in a congealing pool of blood in the Rumpus Room, Mason had time to think. He thought and planned for much of the night. When morning peeked through the windows, he went driving. Dawn was when the homeless people left the underpasses and alleys, or the shelters if they were lucky, and claimed their corners for the day.

By six thirty, Mason was back, with a passenger.

By seven o'clock, the homeless man, roughly Mason's height and build, was dead.

By eight o'clock, Mason had gathered into a backpack and a duffel bag the things he wanted to take with him. That included wads of cash that Sonya had yet to deposit, and the fake ID that she had paid for the year before.

As she and Monica had become busier, more responsibilities fell upon Mason's shoulders, including running errands and purchasing supplies, which often included alcohol. The fake driver's license had saved her a lot of time in the long run, since neither she nor Monica would have to be bothered with these errands. He never knew where the name Jack Ferris had come from, but from this point on, it would be his.

His preparations made, he lay down on his bed and waited.

At nine o'clock, he took a deep breath and stood up.

He went into the Rumpus Room, careful to stay out of the blood. He looked at the strange and gruesome tableau spread out before him. The homeless man, his throat cut, lay at Sonya and

181

Monica's feet. Sonya, still lying on her side, naked except for the arrangement of leather straps and the fake orange-brown wig. Monica, lying on her back, in a similar outfit and a yellow wig.

Then, there were the candles that Mason had arranged around them, and the piles of wadded up newspapers filling the space in the middle of the bodies, and between the bodies and the candles. He hoped he had thought of everything. He had seen enough crime shows on TV to know that crime scene investigation had become quite sophisticated in recent years.

He didn't want this to look like a crime scene, but like a sex ritual gone horribly awry.

He peered at Monica's face, burning it into his memory. He had thought about taking the wig off of her, but he decided to keep the scene as accurate and genuine as possible. He felt tears welling up in his eyes as he looked at her. He shook his head and blinked them away.

Then he looked at his mother. Sonya looked so small, her knees still bent from her kneeling posture. Mason thought she looked somewhat bizarre, not only from the look of surprise frozen on her face, but also from the skin having stretched in places where the smeared blood had dried.

As he stood there surveying the scene, Mason received a message. "It's time," he heard.

"I know," he replied.

He took a lighter from his pocket and lit the newspapers in several spots around the bodies, then he stood back. The newspapers quickly turned into an intense conflagration, engulfing the bodies, melting the sheet of plastic under them, catching the carpet on fire. In no time, the wall was burning, as was the floor.

Mason slowly stepped back toward the door, keeping an eye on his work, making sure it burned sufficiently.

A few hours before, he had thought about doing this during the night, but he decided to wait until daylight. He knew that the flames would be much more visible at night. In the daylight, he hoped that the flames would not be as noticeable until it was too late. And waiting until after nine o'clock, he reasoned, would mean that people would be at work, with fewer around to see the fire and report it.

In just a few minutes, the flames had crept to the bed, which was now fully engulfed. Curtains, walls, furnishings, even the ceiling, all had flames licking across them. As the blaze made its way toward the door, Mason kept backing away, squinting as waves of heat blew his hair and clothing.

He could not even see the bodies any longer, and was satisfied with his preparations. Once outside the room, in the hallway, he picked up his backpack and the duffel bag from where he had left them, and slipped out the back door of the house. He walked away on foot, leaving Sonya's car, and Monica's, parked in the garage.

arker walked in the door and found Hunter and Lily in the family room, sitting by the fire. They were both watching the flames and hadn't heard him come in.

Parker tossed his keys noisily on the end table.

"Hey, there he is," Hunter said, as they both turned at the startling sound. "Good thing you finally arrived. Lily's fading."

Lily smiled a weary smile. "I'm okay," she said, "just kind of tired."

"Yeah, I thought I was going to have to put her to bed myself," Hunter joked.

Parker wasn't amused.

As Lily struggled to her feet, Hunter took her arm and helped her up. She did a friendly wave toward Hunter and walked toward Parker. He put a hand tentatively on her shoulder.

"I really am okay," she said. Then, with a puzzled expression, she asked, "Are you?"

"Yeah," he said. "I'm sorry, baby. I just didn't realize it was getting so late."

"That's fine," she reassured him. "I'm going to bed now."

"Okay, hon," he answered with a quick kiss. "Sleep well."

He watched her head down the hall toward the bedroom, then he turned his attention to Hunter who was walking toward him. The embers of his anger were simmering again.

"You still say there's nothing going on here?" Parker asked quietly.

Hunter stopped in his tracks and looked at Parker through narrowed eyes.

"What?" Hunter asked. "Are you back on that again?"

Parker glanced down the hallway, then he motioned for Hunter to follow him out to the back patio, to keep from being overheard. The sun was going down, but he didn't turn the light on.

"Well, you can't seem to stay away from Lily!" Parker said once they were outside.

"Oh come on, Parker. Don't be such a horse's ass. I came over to talk about the case."

"I know. That's always your excuse lately."

"Okay," Hunter said, the anger in his voice apparent despite keeping his volume low, "one, you've admitted you don't even love Lily anymore. So even if I *was* interested in her, so what? Two, you've already got somebody else lined up, so I say again, even if I *was* interested in Lily, so what? And three, she's actually been remembering things about that day. Things that she's had locked away for three years. And instead of making her worse, she actually seems to be opening up a little, getting a little better. And I admire that little lady a lot, and we ain't involved. But even if we were, so the fuck what?"

"Bullshit."

"Bullshit, what? Name one of those things I said that ain't true!"

"You just look for opportunities to be alone with her. Coming over here when I'm gone, taking her driving to the crime scene."

"Oh yeah," Hunter said. "Talk about romance! I take her over to the neighborhood where she was tied up and her best friend was murdered in front of her, and she's all over me! Nothing like a horrible bloody memory to get the sparks flying!"

"You haven't denied you're trying to spend time alone with her."

186

"Alright, you asshole," Hunter said, giving in to the anger, "I thought you'd be home before now, and incidentally so did Lily. And you want to come driving with us, retracing that day, you're more than welcome."

Parker felt his argument losing steam. He put both hands up to rub his face, and he sighed in frustration, throwing himself down on one of the wrought iron chairs with a grunt. He was reminded, too late, that they had already taken the cushions in for the season. He winced at the hard cold metal on his back and tailbone. Hunter watched him with a bewildered expression and shook his head.

"What the hell's wrong with you?" he asked.

Parker looked up at him for a few seconds, feeling suddenly exhausted.

"You know that woman that signed me up for the calendar?" he finally responded. Hunter nodded. "She wants me to do more modeling, and we met this afternoon to talk about the jobs she's already got lined up for me." He paused, and sighed again. "We ended up having sex."

Hunter turned to face him squarely, cocking his head to the side and looking down at him with a critical look.

"So not only were you unfaithful to Lily, you were unfaithful to Kenzie, too."

"Yeah, thanks for pointing out the obvious, Hunt." His tone was biting, but he was more angry at himself.

"And you had the nerve to get mad at me because you thought *I* was interested in Lily? You know, sometimes I think your truck's got a higher IQ than you do."

Parker turned his head away, simmering in his shame.

"So, what are you going to do?" Hunter asked.

"What am I going to do about what?"

"About what? About what you just told me. About Lily. About Kenzie. About this new woman."

"There's nothing to do about the new woman," Parker said. "There's not a relationship there. She just wanted sex."

"Are you sure? Because I think you're thinking about men. Women usually want more than just sex."

Parker thought for a moment, decided he didn't have an answer, and decided instead to respond to an earlier question of Hunter's.

"I don't know why I'm getting so weird about Lily. I still feel the same way I did the last time we talked about this. I don't know. My life just feels so fucked up right now."

"Yeah, really fucked up!" Hunter replied with a sarcastic edge. "You've got a successful construction business. On top of that, you're getting modeling jobs. You've got *three* good-looking women interested in you. Damn, little brother, I don't know how you can stand being in this puddle of shit."

"You just don't understand."

"No, I don't. I don't understand how, with all that going for you, you can think your life is so fucked up. You know, from my point of view, you've got it good. For me, it's pretty simple. All I want is to have my wife back."

Parker looked up at him, shame etched in his face.

"Aw, Hunter, I'm sorry. I didn't mean – "

Hunter put his hand up and cut him off.

"You know what, Parker? Just forget it. You're a hot mess and I just don't have what it takes to deal with you now."

Hunter turned toward the door. Hearing the scuff of his shoes as he stopped abruptly, Parker looked up.

"Lily!" Hunter said, and Parker suddenly felt his heart in his throat. As he saw the stricken look on Lily's face as she looked out the partly open window of their bedroom, he knew he really *was* a shit.

Kenzie held on to her determination to tell Jim about her plans to go to North Carolina with JuleighAnn. She held tightly to it as she drove back home. She held on to it during their Saturday afternoon lovemaking session.

She was still holding on to it when she was lying in bed at eight thirty, listening to Jim snore.

Still awake at nine o'clock, she decided to get up for a while. Jim's snoring remained undisturbed as she got out of bed, put on a robe and left the room, quietly closing the door behind her. Once she was downstairs again, she unlocked her phone and started up the Facebook app. She saw that there was a message and touched the Messenger icon.

"Sure do miss you," was the message waiting for her from Parker.

"I miss you too, honey," she replied, hoping he was still up to be notified of her response.

Sure enough, seconds later, he was online.

"Hey, baby," he replied, "where you been?"

"I have to go to bed when Jim does. Do you need to chat, or do you want to Skype?"

In less than a minute, they were face to virtual face. Parker noticed immediately her stressed expression and the tension in her voice.

"What's wrong, baby?" he asked.

Kenzie paused for a moment, trying to hold back the tears.

"Jim's made some rules," she replied, her face hard. "I have to go to bed when he does, at eight o'clock, and I can't take my birth control pills anymore. He thinks it's time we have a baby. I hoped to chat with you about it this afternoon, before Jim got back home, but you never responded."

"Yeah, I'm sorry about that. I had some work stuff to take care of."

As Kenzie was wiping her eyes with a tissue, she missed the brief sheepish expression that flashed across his face.

"I've missed you, though," he continued. "I was hoping to chat earlier this evening, but something came up. We haven't had a chance to chat since yesterday, when you told me you got my check."

"I know. Jim laid down the law as soon as I got home from work yesterday."

"I'm sorry, honey. Well, have you decided when you're going to come out here?"

"Not yet," Kenzie said, feeling again the nervousness that she had been feeling all afternoon. "I have the plan all worked out, but I just need to schedule it. And tell Jim."

"Tell me what?" Jim asked from the stairway. Kenzie jumped, her heart suddenly hammering against her rib cage. "And what is it that you're planning?"

In a panic, and without a word to Parker, Kenzie quickly disconnected and quit Skype as Jim came the rest of the way down the stairs.

"I thought we agreed that you go to bed when I do," he said as he approached.

"I did, Jim," Kenzie replied, her voice quivering, "but I couldn't sleep. So I just got up a few minutes ago."

"Uh huh," Jim said, unfazed by her explanation. "And then I come down here to find you chatting up some guy, making plans that you haven't told me about yet. One of the rules was no more staying up late to chat on Facebook." By now, he was standing directly in front of her. "So who was that, Kenzie? Was it Brad?"

"No, it was JuleighAnn," Kenzie said quietly. Jim narrowed his eyes as he looked at her, but Kenzie didn't see it. She was looking down at the cell phone in her hands. "She's going out east for a few days and invited me to come along."

"That wasn't JuleighAnn," Jim said angrily. "That was a man's voice!"

"No, it was just a bad connection." Kenzie amazed herself at how quickly she came up with the lie. She was proud of herself, and a little ashamed at the same time.

"You said you have to schedule it. If it's JuleighAnn's trip, isn't it already scheduled?"

"I meant I need to schedule the time off from work."

"You're full of shit!" Jim snatched the phone out of her hands. He touched the face of it to wake it up and saw the blank for a password to be entered. "Password protected now? What the fuck don't you want me to see?"

"It's nothing," Kenzie said, trying to make her voice sound casual, but not at all happy with the results.

"If it's nothing, then why won't you tell me?" He paused for a response, then continued when there was none. "What the fuck is your password?"

"Jim, why are you doing this?" Kenzie asked as she emotionally sank into the sofa.

"Are you having an affair?" Jim asked quite loudly, ignoring her question. By now he was leaning over her.

"Jim," Kenzie whimpered, putting her hands up to her ears.

"Are you fucking somebody else?" he yelled. He grabbed one of her hands, also grabbing a handful of her abundant hair with it. When this resulted in her head being yanked violently to the side, she screamed. Her scream startled him and he let go, but he stood there looking at her, huffing angrily.

Finally, needing to give his anger an outlet, he hurled her phone across the room where it smashed against the brick fireplace. Then he turned and stomped across the living room and up the stairs, uttering a sound that very much resembled a growl.

Kenzie heard the bedroom door slam and, her body shaking from the fear, she pushed herself up from the sofa and walked unsteadily to the fireplace. The face of her phone was shattered, the back was off, and broken pieces of the electronic innards were scattered about her.

Kneeling on the floor, she put her head down and sobbed.

Thinking back, Mason was still happy with the effectiveness of his plans. His reasoning during that night so long ago had proved valid. Even though he had made his escape on foot, walking casually so as not to attract attention, he was already more than a mile away when he heard the first siren heading toward the house.

And when he checked the newspaper in the days that followed, he saw that the investigation had revealed there were no accelerants present, and that the source of the fire was apparently a number of candles in the bedroom. The cause of the fire was ruled as accidental. All three occupants of the house were killed, though the media had a field day with conjecture on what the trio might have been involved in together in that bedroom.

Neighbors had been interviewed, and a profile was created of the three people who had lived in the house. They generally seemed nice, but kept to themselves. The two women were described by different neighbors as hot or sexy, one woman calling them sluts. They appeared to be lovers, but there were other individuals, usually men, who showed up at various times. A few leering suggestions were made, but nobody had any proof.

The boy had always been polite, a very sweet kid. It was so sad that he had been involved with these nefarious women.

The house had fallen in on the victims, and by the time it had burned itself out, there was little left. Investigators found the three bodies, but having already gathered information about the residents, no additional effort was expended to try to identify them.

Mason shed the cloak of Mason Dodd, fully becoming Jack Ferris. He resumed the nomadic lifestyle that he had known in his earlier years, picking up odd jobs here and there, or living off Sonya's cash when he couldn't find one, staying in a town until he felt impelled to move. Or until he saw a woman whose auburn hair resurrected the mental effigy he carried with him of Sonya in that wig.

Even though he felt helpless against the messages, the voices that drove him to kill his mother again, he was always extremely careful with the implementation. He never left any clues behind, and once the deed was done, he didn't stick around. He didn't panic, but he wasn't narcissistic, so he didn't stay to follow the investigation, either.

And all those years, he had been successful. At least until three years ago in Raleigh, North Carolina. Not that he had ever been a suspect in the murder. But several things had gone wrong.

His first mistake had been taking two women at once. But it was the first time he had come across two women together who brought back Sonya *and* Monica as he last saw them.

It had started out easy enough. Following them in a taxi to the shopping center, then waiting for them. It was a hot day, made even hotter by the Edward Scissorhands outfit, so he found some shade while he kept an eye on the doors they had entered.

Slipping into the back seat after they got in the car was a piece of cake. Women never pay that much attention to their surroundings in a parking lot, especially when they're involved in conversation with a friend. Having donned the spandex hood that he had taken from Sonya's collection, the one with the zippered eye and mouth openings, as well as latex gloves, he was confident knowing that he was completely covered and left no physical evidence behind.

Convincing the 'Sonya' woman to drive to the house was also easy, once they saw the gun. He had discovered the house on the lawn mowing circuit with the company he had been working for. He had heard that the owners were on vacation and that it would be vacant. Having ascertained there was no alarm system, and noticing the privacy of the property, and of others in the neighborhood, it was easy enough to break in and make his preparations.

Imagine the owners' surprise when they returned to find that their home was the scene of a bloody murder!

Once inside the house, it had been easy, at gunpoint, to force the 'Sonya' woman to tie up the 'Monica' woman, although in retrospect, he should have inspected the zip ties a little more closely than he had. She was in a dining room chair, facing the table a few feet away.

'Sonya' had struggled with him when he tried to tie her to the table and, as was often the case, required a few blows with the butt of the pistol to take the fight out of her. Killing 'Sonya' went as per usual, with her pleading and screaming turning to a gurgling hiss when her throat was cut. However, 'Monica' continued screaming and crying, which Mason found to be extremely annoying. Turned out she wasn't at all like Monica. She was so irritating! When he approached her to silence her, everything went to hell.

She had managed to work one hand free, then the other one. Looking back, despite the amount of trouble she caused him, he had to admire the coolness and effectiveness of her actions after that. Although he hadn't seen it happen, apparently she had tipped the chair back, sliding the chair legs out of the zip ties that attached her ankles to it.

His first intimation that anything was wrong was when she stood up, picked up the chair and swung it at him. He saw it in enough time to deflect the blow with his arm, but still, the glancing blow against the side of his head knocked him senseless for a moment.

Long enough for her to get away.

Cursing his carelessness, he tried to be calm, gathering up everything that he had brought with him, and quietly drove away in his old Dodge Dart that he had left in the garage.

He should have just left Raleigh right then. Just cut his losses and drove away. But he didn't. His car was packed and ready to go, and he was planning to leave the next day. But that night, still kicking himself about what went wrong, he was distracted and was involved in a serious accident in which he struck and killed a pedestrian.

He would have made a break for it, except that there just happened to be a police car there at the intersection. Dumb fucking luck!

Though 'Jack Ferris' had no previous record, and his fingerprints were not on file, he was sentenced to three years for vehicular manslaughter in relation to the accident. Having served two years and a few months, he was released a few weeks ago for good behavior.

"You should track down 'Monica' and get rid of her!"

"She obviously doesn't know anything. Don't worry about it."

"But what if she remembers something?"

"You should just get out of here!"

The messages in his head were contradictory. In the end, it was up to Jack to decide. He decided to stick around long enough to cover his tracks.

Kenzie woke up on the sofa with sunlight on her face. After Jim had shattered her phone in a fit of rage, she was angry and afraid of him. She couldn't go to bed with him. Since he hadn't come back looking for her, she assumed that he apparently had been okay with the sleeping arrangements, too.

For now, at least.

She noticed the marks on her wrist where Jim had grabbed her last night. She rubbed her fingers gently across the marks, clearly showing the grip of his fingers. The side of her head was still a little tender, too, where he had yanked her hair along with her wrist.

She looked at her watch. It was almost eight thirty. Jim was always up way before that, even on Sunday. A quick inspection of the house revealed he was gone, and a feeling of relief engulfed her.

And a feeling of dread for when he came back.

She stood in the bedroom for a moment, trying to think. She felt a stressful pounding in her head. In a mental fog, she took off her robe and nightgown and got dressed.

Experiencing a mixture of lethargy and despair, she briefly, slowly, wandered around the house. Several times, she wiped tears from her eyes, and felt angry that they kept coming back. She didn't know what to do with herself.

Until she dragged her feet into the kitchen and saw the coffee maker. Making coffee helped her to focus her thoughts and attention on something for a few minutes. She was barely aware of the minutes that passed as the coffee brewed and she stood at the counter watching the coffee maker. But when she finally poured a cup, the smell and taste helped even more.

She went back into the living room, sipping her coffee. Seeing the pieces of her phone on the coffee table, her thoughts were suddenly galvanized into the beginnings of a plan. She set her coffee cup beside the phone remnants and went back into the kitchen. Picking a business card out of the book she kept by the phone, she lifted the receiver of the wall phone.

After dialing a number, she waited, blowing a disappointed sigh, while listening to a voice mail greeting.

"Brad," she said after the tone, "it's Kenzie. I need to speak with you as soon as possible. Please give me a call at my home phone. Thanks."

After hanging up, she went to the coat closet, fishing out a bag hanging on a hook. She took it back with her into the kitchen, and pulling out her laptop, she plugged it in beside the kitchen table. Since she had started using the smart phone apps, she had gradually used the computer less and less, aside from Skyping with Parker a couple of times. And even that she had done a number of times on her phone.

She started up Facebook and logged in. Parker wasn't online, but she knew that he could come online right away, if his phone buzzed when her message showed up.

"Hey babe," she typed, "are you there?"

Sure enough, a few seconds later, she saw that he was online and typing.

"Good morning, sweetie. How are you? Are you alright?"

"No, I'm not. Jim caught me Skyping with you last night. He and I had another fight. I slept on the sofa."

A few seconds passed between when he saw her message and when he started responding.

"Wow! That's weird timing. I'm kind of in the dog house, too. Lily and I had a fight last night, before I Skyped with you. But you and I were interrupted before I could get to that."

"Really?" Kenzie replied. She thought for a few moments. "I'm surprised. I've always gotten the impression from you that, with her depression, she was somewhat weak and impassive, not much of a fighter."

"Yeah, well lately, she's been sort of coming out of it. I mean, she still has a long way to go, but my brother's been spending some time with her. She seems to be responding to that."

Kenzie read his message a couple of times before she replied.

"Does that mean what I think it means?"

"He insists it doesn't, that he's not interested in her. But I see how she's been acting lately, when he's around."

"Well, that's good, isn't it?" Kenzie asked. "You've been worried about breaking up with her in her condition. Now, you won't be leaving her alone, and she'll have someone to take care of her."

"Yeah."

Kenzie waited a bit, but he gave no follow up remark.

"Is that what the fight was about?" she finally asked.

"No, actually it was about you. Hunter and I were on the back patio talking about me leaving her for you. She overheard that."

"Oh shit." She felt as if her heart dropped into her stomach. "Parker, I'm so sorry!"

"It's okay, babe. It's not your fault."

"I feel like a home wrecker. I'm the other woman."

"No, Kenzie. You're not a home wrecker. Lily and I have been heading down this road for a while now. You just happened to come along when we reached the end."

Kenzie read his message a couple of times, trying to let it make her feel better, but it was taking some time. Parker filled the gap.

"Anyway, I'm actually packing up some stuff to move out. Joe, a guy on my crew, told me about a vacancy in the building he's in, so I took it."

Kenzie felt a strange ripple in her chest, a feeling of excitement, replacing the shitty one that was there a moment ago. A number of thoughts tumbled through her mind, and she grabbed onto the most prominent one of them. Parker's free. Now, when she goes out there for her visit, Kenzie won't have to stay in a hotel room all by herself. Things were beginning to work out as they had hoped!

"What about you?" Parker asked after a pause. "What was your fight with Jim about? Does he know about us?"

Kenzie sighed, reluctant to think about it again, but knowing she needed to.

"No," she replied. "I told him I was talking to a friend here in town. He didn't really believe me. He heard a man's voice. He's suspicious that it's Brad, my manager at work." She paused, took a deep breath, and continued typing. "He yelled at me for a few minutes, then he smashed my phone."

"Oh my god, Kenzie!" Parker replied. "You have to get away from him!"

"I know. I have a call in to Brad. I'm going to take a week off and go out to North Carolina and see what all the fuss is about."

"This week?"

"Yes, if it works for you. I wanted to check with you before I booked a flight."

"Absolutely, honey! I'd love to see you face to face, be able to hold you in my arms."

Kenzie felt that nervous flutter again, the warm flush that she had been feeling with Parker lately.

"Good," she typed, smiling. "I'll get out of Facebook and see what kind of deal I can get on airfare."

"Okay, sweetie, I can't wait!"

"I'll let you know as soon as I get something booked."

"I love you, baby!" he said.

Kenzie smiled, gazing at those words.

"I love you, too," she typed.

With a sigh, she left Facebook and went to the Expedia web site. Just as the page was loading, the phone rang.

"Hello?"

"Hi, Kenzie, it's Brad. I'm returning your call."

"Hi Brad. I just needed to let you know that, well, I know it's really short notice, and I'm sorry, but I need to take this week off."

"This week? Starting tomorrow? Kenzie, I'm sorry, but I'm afraid that won't work. The Sawyer exhibit is opening tomorrow and as you know, we're expecting a big turnout."

"Yes, I know that," she replied, feeling her heart pounding. "And I'm really sorry about this, but I'm not asking. I need to take this time. It's kind of an emergency situation. I just wanted to let you know."

"Kenzie, is everything alright?" he asked, his tone changing to sympathetic. "I know you haven't quite been yourself the past week or two."

She heard a door open and close, and she heard Jim walking toward the kitchen.

"Yes, Brad, I'm fine. I need to do this. I just can't elaborate right now."

Jim was standing in the kitchen door looking at her. She didn't even hear what Brad said in response.

"Thanks, Brad," she said. "Goodbye."

She looked at Jim, thinking she could smell alcohol. Jim's face was cryptic, completely unreadable.

Until she saw the vein in his forehead throbbing.

"So," he said as he started walking slowly toward her, his tone quietly chilling. "The first opportunity you get, you get on the phone with your boyfriend?" He suddenly raised the volume on the last word, and punctuated the sentence with a vicious backhand across the left side of Kenzie's face.

The force of the blow threw her back against a cabinet. She put her hand up to her face where, just below her eye, she already felt a welt rising from Jim's wedding band.

"Jim," Kenzie said shakily, feeling the tears coming, "he's not my boyfriend."

Jim ignored her. He shook his hand, looking at Kenzie with anger as if it was her face's fault that his hand hurt.

"Expedia?" he said when he glanced down at the computer on the table. "Booking a little getaway with loverboy? What the hell are you going to pay for it with?"

She was about to protest the accusation, but she hesitated when she thought about the second question. She realized then that she really hadn't thought that far in advance. Jim was absolutely right. Even her five hundred dollars cash wouldn't do her any good when it came time to book a flight online.

"Jim, there's nothing going on with Brad," she insisted.

"You know," Jim said as he powered down the computer, "I was going to apologize for breaking your phone. But now I see that you just can't be trusted online at all."

Kenzie watched apprehensively as he bent over to unplug it, and she picked the computer up off the table. Jim stood back up with the plug in his hand, and he reached for the computer, but Kenzie turned, keeping it out of his reach.

"Hand it over, Kenzie," he said.

"No, Jim, you can't do this. This is my computer."

"Give me the laptop, Kenzie," he said in a forceful monotone. Kenzie was backing away from him, but in doing so, she trapped herself in the kitchen. Now in the corner, facing the cabinets, she turned her back to Jim, the front of her hips against the edges of the countertop.

Jim reached around her on the right and gripped the laptop, and she tried to turn away from his hand, toward the left. As Jim felt his grip slipping, he reached his left hand around the other side. At that moment, Kenzie succeeded in tearing the computer from him, and the laptop slammed into his left hand, already sore from hitting her in the face. The computer banged hard against his fingers.

"God damn fucking bitch!" Jim yelled, and he grabbed his fingers, wondering in that instant if they had been broken. Kenzie didn't wait to find out. She snatched up the cord and the bag and ran out of the kitchen. At the front door, she grabbed her purse and a jacket and left.

ily sat in an overstuffed armchair, pressing a wadded up tissue against her eyes. The tissue was nearly spent, damp all the way through. Lily was in the comfortable room that Jane, her therapist, used to see clients. After Parker had left last night, Lily placed the call and Jane had made time for her.

Jane was a middle-aged woman with soft, motherly features, a common-looking but friendly face that tended to help her clients open up.

"So Parker's gone?" she asked.

"Yes," Lily nodded. "He packed up a few things and went to Joe's place. Joe's one of the guys who works for him. There's a vacant apartment in his building, but Parker can't sign the paperwork until the leasing office opens tomorrow morning. So he's crashing on Joe's sofa until then."

"Lily, I'm so sorry to hear this. I know it's come as a shock. I have to say, though, that in spite of this recent turn of events, I'm very impressed with how you're holding up."

"Thanks," Lily sniffed, studying the damp wad in her hands. She thought for a few seconds, then looked at Jane. "Recently, I've been feeling better than I have in the last three years. The time that Hunter spent with me, retracing that horrible day, was oddly comforting. I mean the memories that came back to me aren't pleasant by any means. They're not even necessarily help-ful as far as solving Kathy's murder is concerned. But it's kind of reassured me that I might have a chance at being normal again."

Jane turned her head slightly, looking at Lily with a somewhat scolding expression.

"Normal?" she asked, raising her eyebrows.

"I know," Lily replied, cringing a bit.

Jane had maintained that it's completely normal for the brain to protect itself from things that were too painful to remember by blocking them out. It was also perfectly normal to be depressed after the death, especially the violent death, of a close friend.

While those normal reactions should not be allowed to continue indefinitely, they should not make her feel bad about herself. Crazy, psycho, nuts, abnormal – none of those commonly used words applied, and in fact, Jane maintained, could prove detrimental to bettering oneself.

"What I mean is that those normal reactions just don't *feel* normal," Lily continued. "But these last few days, when I started recalling details about that day without breaking down into a weeping, neurotic bundle of nerves, I also began to recognize the return of my confidence. It's been a long time since I've felt that. Obviously it's really tiny doses, but I kind of feel an inner strength that I haven't felt in years."

"How so?"

"Well, I've been outside, in the daylight, and survived. I've revisited the neighborhood where Kathy was murdered and have been able to think clearly about it. I've actually remembered that last ride in Kathy's car, and the killer sitting in the back seat, without collapsing into a fetal position."

Jane nodded and smiled almost imperceptibly.

"I don't know why I still can't picture his face," Lily said, "but hopefully, in time, that will come too.

"But now, I feel like I've lost it again. Like I've taken one step forward and two steps back. The progress I've made has all been snatched away. It's all gone."

She looked at Jane, who had a doubtful look on her face.

"Okay," Lily conceded, "not gone. Seriously hobbled, maybe, but not erased."

Jane nodded her agreement.

"The fact that you drove yourself here, despite these latest developments, is proof of that."

"Yeah, I guess." Lily tossed the tissue in the little trash can beside the chair and snatched another one from the box.

"So, about these latest developments, how are you dealing with that?"

Tears flooded Lily's eyes again as she thought about last night.

"Damn Parker!" she said. She was going for vehemence, but only managed something that sounded like tired annoyance. Irritated, she stood up and paced around the little room. "He was always so loyal, so supportive. Now, when I really need him, he betrays me. Twice! First, with an emotional affair online, and then by fucking a woman in a local hotel."

"You know what I'm seeing?" Jane asked. "Your pacing, your anger. Obviously what Parker did is not a good thing, but your reaction to it is *very* good, very encouraging. Very *normal.*"

Lily scoffed, but she allowed a slight smile at Jane's use of the word. She thought back to their argument last night, after she had overheard that awful conversation between Parker and Hunter.

"I'm amazed now that I actually had an argument in me last night."

"Yes, that's another example of what I'm talking about."

"Honestly, it wasn't much of a fight," Lily said. "I confronted Parker about those two women and he admitted his guilt, along with the fact that he doesn't love me anymore. I cried and told him to get out, and he agreed." She wiped her eyes again.

"But for you, Lily," Jane said, leaving the statement open, encouraging Lily's acceptance.

"I know." Lily stood at the window where the blinds were tilted most of the way closed, and she peeked through the crack. "That streamlined version of a fight left me exhausted, but again, it gave an odd boost to my confidence level." She turned from the window and plopped back down in the chair. "At the same time, it made me feel lost and forsaken."

"Understandable, under the circumstances."

"And Hunter!" Lily said. "I thought about him later. He excused himself pretty much right away, but thinking back to his exchange with Parker out on the patio, I realized that he knew about that Kenzie woman for a while. He certainly knew when he had spent that time with me revisiting Kathy's last day. He knew about Parker's relationship with Kenzie and didn't say a word!"

"They're brothers," Jane said. "I'm certainly not condoning it, but – "

"I know," Lily interrupted. "I understand that bond of loyalty to your sibling. But still, for him to know that Parker was in love with another woman and not tell me, that just makes me feel like a stupid, naïve little child."

Jane raised her eyebrows again, but said nothing.

"I hate them both!" Lily said.

Still, Jane sat there quietly, allowing Lily to express her anger unhindered.

Lily wiped her eyes and her nose, then threw the tissue in the trash can.

"No, I don't," she said with a sigh, leaning her head on the back of the chair. "Not really. I feel betrayed, hurt, lost, abandoned. But I don't hate them. I know I can't have been easy for Parker to deal with." A bitter smile appeared on her face. "In fact, during brief moments of clarity, I realized that I was kind of surprised that he hadn't strayed sooner."

Jane narrowed her eyes as she looked at Lily.

"Just be careful," she suggested softly, "that you don't take responsibility for his actions."

"No, you're right," Lily agreed, "I know it's not my fault that he was unfaithful. He made his own choices. But I wonder: if the tables were turned, would I have made different choices?"

There was a brief silence, then Lily lifted her head and looked at Jane.

"You know what almost hurts worse than that, though?" she asked. "It's how alone I feel. My best friend died three years ago, and in the time since, other friends just kind of drifted away the more I retreated into my dark little shell.

"And now I've lost the only other person who still shared my life."

"Well, you know what?" Jane asked. "I'm quite sure that if you reach out to your old friends, at least some of them would be happy to come around again."

unday night, Hunter sat alone in his love seat, his feet up on the coffee table. Alone, because he didn't count Jarvis. The cat was lying on the chair opposite him, motionless, just staring at him with what Hunter interpreted as a chilling expression.

"Plotting how you're going to eat me?" Hunter asked. Jarvis slowly blinked once and continued the stare.

Hunter looked back down at the file in his lap. Once again, he had been unsuccessful at coming closer to a resolution. The entries in the file still remained just a random, apparently unrelated collection of facts. Dissatisfied with the perfect crime scenario, he shook his head as he closed the folder.

He had pored through the folder and his notes numerous times today, and spent time thinking about the cases when he was busy with mundane household duties. It hadn't helped him solve the case yet, but it did help him to keep his mind off of what happened last night.

With the reminder of it now, he sighed and shook his head. The expression he had seen on Lily's face after she had overheard his conversation with Parker broke his heart.

Knowing what she had endured and witnessed at the hands of the killer, and how it had affected her emotional and mental health since then, he had been particularly pleased with how she had been able to help him reconstruct Kathy's final day. While she hadn't remembered any significant clues, he hoped that eventually something might shake loose.

Now, though, Lily was pissed at him. And who could blame her? All the time he had been spending with her, gaining her confidence, and the whole time, he was carrying this major, life-changing bit of information and didn't see fit to tell her.

Yeah, yeah, there was that whole 'blood is thicker than water' philosophy. Loyalty to a brother trumps loyalty to somebody outside the bounds of blood relations. But still, he could understand her being upset at him.

And seeing her face. The hurt, the sadness. And knowing that he was one of the two people who had put that look on her face. Her trust in him was shattered, almost as much as her trust in Parker. How long would it take for him to regain her trust to the level it was at before? Would she even allow it at all?

He looked down and noticed he was scratching his wrists. They were already red and irritated, and he wondered how long he had been doing it. He forced himself to stop.

He took the file folder from his lap and laid it on the end table, on top of his laptop. He kept the laptop there so it would always be within easy reach, and as he saw it, he had an idea.

R.J. had said there had been no similar murders, but Hunter decided to check for himself. Again, he was grasping at straws, but sooner or later, one of those straws had to be connected to something.

He logged into the police department's database, using R.J.'s password. R.J. wasn't aware that Hunter had seen him type it, and Hunter didn't see any need to tell him.

He typed in a few key words to search for, including 'throat slash' and 'auburn hair' and 'unsolved.' He hit the Enter key before he realized that he forgot to type 'North Carolina.'

"Stupid," he said out loud. He was about to add those two words to the search string, when the list that appeared caught his eye. He saw a listing for Kathy's murder, and a brief entry of Jenny Norbert's. Besides them, five similar murders in the last fifteen years remained unsolved. Hunter didn't have access to the complete reports online, but he read the synopsis that accompanied each heading. The first was in Philadelphia, followed by York, Pennsylvania, then Columbia, Maryland, Harrisonburg, Virginia and Greensboro, North Carolina. Followed, of course, by two in Raleigh, North Carolina, three years apart.

Each victim was a woman with auburn hair, each was tied to the top of a dining room table with nylon zip ties, each had her throat cut, and each murder scene was clean of any physical evidence and lacking a viable suspect. Hunter opened a Google map page and looked at the locations. The murders occurred chronologically in a rough line leading to Raleigh.

As the murders were separated by a distance of fifty miles, and sometimes quite a bit more, likely nobody had made a connection. And even if there *was* a connection, so what? There was not a single suspect between them.

Still, this was a development that had to be considered. In the hopes that R.J. could get copies of the police files, Hunter took down notes of the pertinent information.

A squirrel sat on a chunk of granite as he busily chewed on a sunflower seed. He was aware of the rabbit inspecting the ground to his left, but paid as little attention to him as he did to the flickers pecking and digging in the ground for worms and insects.

To the west, the mountains wore a mantle of lavender alpenglow as the sun cleared the horizon far to the east. The air was suffused with a fresh, distinctive scent, a combination of morning dew and pine trees.

Startled by a sound behind him, the squirrel abandoned his rock and hastily scratched his way up the trunk of a linden tree. The flickers flew away to resume their hunts in different lawns, but the rabbit waited. His muscles quivering, tensed and ready for flight, he continued his chewing as he turned his head in the direction of the sound.

The front door opened and Kenzie walked outside, followed by JuleighAnn and Arden. Arden was holding Kenzie's laptop in one hand, but he quickly closed the door before Molson could follow them out. The dog watched through the glass, appearing indignant at being excluded.

"Oh," Kenzie said in that high-pitched voice women use when talking about babies and small animals, "look how cute!" She smiled as the rabbit warily made his way under the hedge at the edge of the yard.

She looked around, taking in her surroundings with an eye that knew it may not behold them for a long while. She inhaled deeply and sighed.

"I love that smell!"

When she turned toward JuleighAnn and Arden, she had tears in her eyes. Her left cheek, up to her eye, was purple where Jim had hit her. In the middle of the purple was a cut from his wedding band that JuleighAnn had bandaged.

"Please be careful," JuleighAnn said with a worried tone in her voice. Kenzie nodded, biting her lip. "I may not agree with what you're doing, but I told you I'm behind you in whatever you decide. I meant that."

Kenzie threw her arms around JuleighAnn, closing her eyes tightly against the tears. When they parted, JuleighAnn's eyes were saturated as well. Kenzie moved toward Arden and gave him a hug.

"Take it easy, kiddo," he said. When Kenzie pulled away, Arden had a bewildered look on his face. "Did I really just call you 'kiddo'? I'm not *really* an old fart."

"Hush, honey," JuleighAnn said quietly. "Yes, you are."

Arden smirked in her direction. Then he held out Kenzie's laptop, which she took from him.

"Good luck," he said.

"Thank you both," Kenzie said, and before the tears could spill out of her eyes, she turned and stepped down off the porch. She got in her car and, with one last look toward JuleighAnn and Arden, she drove away.

It was early, well before rush hour, but it was still a good half-hour drive toward her home. During the drive, she thought about all that had happened in the last few hours.

When she left Jim the night before, Kenzie had driven straight to JuleighAnn, who welcomed her with open arms. After Kenzie related to her and Arden what had happened, they gave her some

216

privacy while she started up her computer and went on Facebook. Parker responded immediately.

"Well, Parker," Kenzie typed, "I did it. I left Jim."

"Really? Are you okay?"

"No, but I will be. He hit me. I've finally had enough."

"The son of a bitch hit you?"

"Yes. I'll be fine, though. I'm at a friend's house. I can't stay on long, but I wanted to let you know that my plans have changed. I'm going to drive out there. And I won't be coming back."

"Kenzie, are you sure?"

"Yes, I am. If you still want me."

There was a pause after her message, and Kenzie hoped it was a good pause, as Parker tried to catch his breath after hearing the good news. She imagined him doing a little happy dance, though she knew that was unlikely. He didn't seem like the happy dance type. She didn't have to wait long to find out.

"My god, Kenzie! Yes, I still want you! Are you kidding?"

She had smiled a relieved smile when she read it.

"Good!" she replied. "I'm going to start out early tomorrow. I'll stop at home first, after Jim has gone to work. I'll pack my clothes and then I'll be on my way."

"Wow! I can't believe it's working out for us. So you'll be here Wednesday?"

"I haven't really mapped it out. I know it's twenty-four hours of driving. I might be able to do it in two days if I make them long days. But I'll just have to see where I can stop for the night, what's halfway."

"Give me a call when you're getting close."

"I can't give you a call," Kenzie replied. "Jim broke my phone last night. And I won't be able to get a new phone till I get where I'm going, and have an address and income."

"Oh, that's right."

"But I'll Skype you from the hotel when I stop for the night. When I see how far I got, I might have a better idea of when I'll be there."

"Sounds good. Whenever you get in town, I'll meet you at The Sawmill. I'll get the address and send it to you. It's a bar Hunter and I go to. It's kind of rowdy, but it's right off the highway and easy to find. We can have a drink, maybe some dinner if you're hungry, and then you can follow me to my place. I'll be in my apartment by then."

Kenzie had smiled as she thought for a moment. Then she started typing.

"A few weeks ago, there was a lot separating us. It seemed impossible. But now, all that's separating us is 1,684 miles! And I'll cross that in two or three days!"

"Baby, I can't wait to see you!" Parker replied. "I'm actually going to be able to hold you in my arms and kiss you!"

"I know." If she had said the words out loud, they likely would have been uttered with the same dreamy quality that adorned her face as she typed them.

After reluctantly bidding Parker good night, Kenzie used JuleighAnn's phone and called Brad, informing him that she was, in fact, quitting her job. She didn't bother to give details, just cited personal issues.

Though she had been exceedingly apologetic, Brad sounded indignant, almost bullying, until Kenzie convinced him that she would not be dissuaded. She wouldn't have bothered to stay on with him that long, except that she arranged to have her final pay held, to forward to her once she arrives at her final destination. She was only sorry she hadn't been able to say goodbye to Betty and Carl, the owners of the gallery.

Now, this morning, Kenzie approached her home cautiously. It was nearly six o'clock, and Jim should be at work. She only hoped that he hadn't realized their situation was as serious as it really was. If he had stayed home from work, her plans would be put on hold.

She pushed the button on the garage door opener remote and watched hopefully. As the door cranked up, she saw that the garage was empty. Breathing a sigh of relief, she pulled into the garage and closed the door.

Kenzie remembered movies that showed women packing to make a hasty retreat. She had always joked about how unrealistic it was, a woman throwing clothes haphazardly into a suitcase and being gone in ten minutes or less.

Now, she decided it wasn't so unrealistic after all. Though she did take longer than ten minutes.

The bed became her base of operation. Jim's side had obviously been slept in, the covers left rumpled and wadded up, while Kenzie's side was still untouched. She carried a set of suitcases up from the basement and opened them up on her side of the bed. She stared at them for a moment, then got busy.

She gathered all her clothes and stuffed them as quickly as she could into the suitcases. She scooped up her toiletries, hair dryer, and various other necessities. She ran around the house selecting other items she wanted to take with her, including favorite books and photographs of family and friends. She realized that the suitcases would not be enough, so she supplemented them with a couple of cardboard boxes from the garage.

Once she had everything packed and loaded in her car, she took a deep breath and looked around more slowly, wanting to make sure she didn't leave anything behind that she really needed. A memory came crashing into her head with a jolt of adrenaline, and she rushed upstairs and into the bedroom. She slipped her hand under the mattress on her side, pulling out the five one hundred dollar bills.

She went back downstairs and put the money in her purse. Finally, she got a sheet of paper and a pen.

Jim,

By the time you see this, I will be far away. Don't bother filing a missing person report. Don't bother looking for me. I don't ever want to see you again in my life.

Your emotional – and now physical – abuse of me has been completely undeserved and has gone on much too long. I'm sure you'll just think I'm overreacting, being a stupid woman. Think what you want. I don't care. You won't have me to mistreat any longer. We're through.

Kenzie.

Just the act of writing that note made her heart beat faster, her breaths more shallow. But now, placing it on the kitchen table where Jim would be sure to see it when he walked in gave her an unexpected feeling of strength. She suddenly felt free. She took a deep breath and let it out, and she felt the weight of his abuse peel off of her like an old, worn out, unwanted garment, wadded up at her feet.

Kenzie took her house keys off her key ring and left them on the note. She picked up her purse and went into the garage, opening the door one last time. After backing her car out, she pressed the remote to lower the garage door, then tossed it into the garage before the door came back down.

Backing out of the driveway, she looked around, melancholy, a little regretful. Then she put her car in gear and drove away.

In minutes, she was on E-470 heading east into the sun, and her regret had turned into hope.

Hunter sat at a small table in the back of The Sawmill, near the pool tables which were not currently in use. The jukebox wasn't blaring, either. It was one o'clock on Monday afternoon. It wouldn't start getting loud and rowdy for another three hours or so.

The file folder in front of him was getting pretty ratty from his daily handling of it. But, in almost a month and a half, it had slowly grown slightly thicker with what information he had been able to add to it. He took a bite of his burger and wiped his hand on his napkin. He washed the bite down with a swallow of beer.

He sensed somebody approaching, and he looked up.

"Hey, R.J.," he said. "Thanks for coming."

"No problem," the detective said. "I'm afraid I haven't got anything new, though. With no new leads on the Norbert case, I've been busy with a couple of other cases."

"That's okay. I might have something."

"Really?" R.J. asked. His interest piqued, he sat down across from Hunter. As he did, the waitress approached.

"Just water for me," he said.

"Oh, come on," Hunter protested. "They make a great cheeseburger."

R.J. looked at Hunter's plate for a moment. Then, without much prodding, he nodded up at the waitress.

"Okay," he said, "I guess I'll have a cheeseburger and fries, and whatever's on tap."

"You got it, hon," the waitress said with a smile, and she shifted her attention to Hunter. She extended the smile for his benefit, and in fact may have even increased it a bit. "You still doing okay?"

"Fine, thanks," Hunter nodded.

"So, what do you have?" R.J. asked after she left.

"Same thing you're having. Cheeseburger and a beer."

"The case, smartass."

"Ah," Hunter said, acting surprised. Suppressing a smile, he opened the folder and pulled out the paper with the details and case file numbers. He handed it to R.J.

"Your handwriting still sucks," R.J. said. "What am I looking at?"

"Five almost identical murders, from Philly to Raleigh. All unsolved."

R.J. looked at the list with a renewed interest.

"Almost identical?" he asked.

"Each victim was a woman with auburn hair, each one was tied to a dining room table, and each one of them had her throat cut."

"And all unsolved?"

"That's right. Just like Kathy's and Jenny Norbert's murders, no physical evidence was found at the scene."

R.J. looked disappointed as he studied the list silently for a while. The waitress brought his beer and set it down in front of him. He nodded at her and took a sip.

"Well?" Hunter finally said.

"I'm not sure what it does for us."

"What are you talking about? It's the first lead we've had in weeks!"

"I don't know how to tell you this, Sherlock, but it's not a lead. If they're all unsolved and none of them have any suspects or clues, then we're no further along than we were."

"I thought you were a detective," Hunter said with an edge to his voice. R.J. rolled his eyes. "It may not tell us who the killer is, but it tells us where he came from. At least starting with the first murder. It tells us the route he took here. It tells us the time-table."

"Yeah, which looking at this, there doesn't seem to be any kind of pattern."

"But maybe if we study it a little more closely, we might be able to find one."

"I don't know," R.J. said doubtfully.

"Look, each of those departments was working their case as if they were isolated murders. None of them knew about the others. They never made the connection, so they didn't realize it was a serial."

"Where'd you get this, anyway?" R.J. asked, fanning the sheet of paper.

"Doesn't matter," Hunter said evasively as he took a bite of his burger.

"Damn it, Hunter, you're going to make me sorry I ever agreed to work with you."

"Not when we solve the cases."

R.J. looked at the list, then back up at Hunter.

"How? What do you expect me to do?"

"Shit, R.J.," Hunter said with an exasperated tone. "I remember when you used to be a cop." He sighed. "Take those case numbers and request copies of the files from the police departments in those cities. Then we can see everything they've got and compare, cross-reference."

R.J. was still balking.

"You know how many active cases I have on my desk now?" he asked.

"So let's solve these and mark them off the list," Hunter said undeterred.

"When the hell am I going to have time to study five more case files?"

"Damn," Hunter said quietly. "For a cop, you sure are unmotivated to do police work."

"I'm sorry, Hunter," R.J. replied equally quietly, his face displaying a modicum of shame. "I've just had enough. I've seen more dead bodies than I care to. And I've seen too many guilty people walk free. I'm seriously thinking of getting out."

"I'm sorry, man. I didn't realize it was getting to you."

"Has been for a while. I can't get away from it. I go home at night and I see the dead bodies in my dreams. Between the dreams and being called to another murder scene, I can't remember the last time I've gotten a full, restful night's sleep." Hunter watched him quietly. R.J. licked his lips as if his mouth was dry, and he took another sip of beer.

"My wife has been encouraging me to quit," he continued, "and lately, that's been sounding pretty damn good. I hate to let you down, Hunter. I know this case is near and dear to your heart."

"Then get the files for me. I'll scour them for clues and connections myself."

R.J. looked at Hunter for a while, at his imploring expression. Then he sighed.

"Alright. I'll call them when I get back after lunch. I'll get you the files."

"Thanks," Hunter said. R.J. shook his head, looking at Hunter sadly.

"But please don't get your hopes up too high, buddy. We got unsolved cases going back decades. These cases kind of have 'unsolved' written all over them."

"I'm not giving up," Hunter said resolutely.

R.J. looked intently into Hunter's eyes, then he nodded.

"I know."

Hunter nodded and smiled, as the waitress approached and placed a plate in front of R.J.

Only then did Hunter realize that he had scratched his wrists raw again.

Mason Dodd, now living under his Jack Ferris persona, was finally happy with the results of his efforts. It had been slow, working with the ancient equipment he had available to him, and with his general unfamiliarity with the internet. But it had finally paid off.

Learning to use the old computer, and the cheap used inkjet printer he had gotten for ten dollars more, had taken precious time. But once he had mastered the learning curve, he was able to get to work.

Privacy laws, unlisted numbers, all had hindered his efforts. It also didn't help that he couldn't focus for very long. After a short time, his thinking would become disorganized, his attention easily diverted, and he would have to stop and sit quietly, sometimes for hours.

During his time in prison, they had kept him drugged, and the unpleasant side effects that he remembered from his teen years returned. The prison doctor had worked with him, trying different medications, which usually meant trading one side effect for another.

Now that he was free again, he was off of that shit and was himself again. And after a couple of weeks of painstaking work, piecing together facts from newspaper articles, cross-referenced with business records that had been filed publicly and various other sources he had stumbled upon, he thought he had finally found what he was looking for.

The diagram he had created on the wall over the computer was evidence of his hard work. Photographs he had printed out, along with excerpts of relevant newspaper articles, maps, random notes, all thumbtacked to the wall in a flowchart that pointed to one destination.

Jack sat back and studied it. He was happy with the harmony of the chart. All the leads he had come across pointed to that one address up in Allure.

Very soon, he could finally be finished and move on.

The first thing he did was quit his job at the diner and collect his pay. He didn't need that shitty job distracting him from his mission.

Then, he spent Monday afternoon driving around, scouting the suburban neighborhood.

When he had gotten out of prison, he was given the few personal effects he had had on him when he was arrested, along with his old Dodge Dart, still packed with his possessions, which had also spent that time incarcerated in the impound lot. Now, after spending the last few weeks either holed up in his apartment or standing at the sink in that greasy spoon washing dishes, it felt good to get out and drive around a little.

He found the address and sat for a while, watching the comings and goings at the house. And he was happy to see there really *weren't* any comings and goings.

Jack left a few times, for food and to use a restroom, and every time he came back, using a different route if possible, the house always looked the same. And only the one car under the carport.

The blinds had been closed all day, and he had begun to wonder if anybody was even there. Maybe they had gone on vacation and wouldn't be back for days. Maybe the information he had found online was old and they had actually moved. Or maybe he just had the wrong information altogether. He had no way to check the license plate of the car parked under the carport, to see who owned it.

But then, his patience was rewarded when he saw the side door open and a woman carried a bag of trash out, placing it in the trash can beside the carport. Jack hadn't wanted to get too close, and from this distance, he couldn't tell for sure, but it looked like her. Her hair was darker now than he remembered it, but still blonde.

He waited longer, as the sun started going down and the neighbors came home from work. But always, it just seemed to be her in that house.

This should be easy.

A short while longer, and he was satisfied. He drove back to his apartment to pack.

Joe and Bud worked alone for about half the day. Parker had stayed behind to sign the paperwork on his apartment, then to run back to the house to get a few more things.

Lily had been sullen when he was there, more than he had ever seen in the last three years. But she had stayed out of his way as he was carrying things to his truck.

She hadn't even made a pretense of having the blinds open when he was there.

Parker was finished before ten o'clock and had carried his things into his apartment. He looked at, and purchased, some used furniture he found on Craigslist, and arranged to come back after work when Joe could help him move it.

In the early afternoon, he rejoined Joe and Bud on the job site, finished out the day, then got the furniture moved into his apartment. It wasn't much, but it was in decent condition. And at least he had a place to sit and a place to sleep.

He hoped Kenzie wouldn't be too turned off by it.

It was a little after nine o'clock, and now with his shower and dinner behind him, he was relaxing on the love seat he had purchased. It had been a busy, stressful day, and he looked forward to getting settled into a new daily routine. Especially once that daily routine included Kenzie.

He hadn't heard from her all day, but he knew she was on the road, without a phone. He longed for her. He couldn't wait to hold her, to feel her body melt against him, to kiss her lips.

Looking at her Facebook pictures again, at her flawless fair skin, her smiling brown eyes, her incredible head of luxuriant red hair, he imagined the warmth of her body, her scent, her taste.

He put his phone back in his pocket, willing her to call.

Kenzie hung the towel over the towel bar and walked into the room where her suitcase was open on the bed. She pulled out her robe and wrapped it around her. She sat down at the requisite motel table and chair arrangement by the window, and in a moment of utter defiance, she didn't even pull her wet hair around, away from the chair.

Fuck Jim! She can do what she wants, now. Including leaving wet marks on the furniture.

She sighed deeply and closed her eyes. It felt good to be away from him. And it felt scary to be on her own, with only the cash she had with her. With food, gas and the motel room, her cash had already decreased significantly. And knowing she didn't have a job to go to when she reached her destination gave her a nagging feeling of trepidation.

She hoped she could get something lined up quickly so she wouldn't be a burden to Parker. That could be tricky, though, knowing the way she had left her job at the gallery. She couldn't be sure if Brad would give her a decent recommendation or not, but she had her doubts.

She opened her eyes and sat forward, waking up her computer on the table. She started up Skype, selected Parker and pressed the video call button. She waited and within a few seconds, he answered.

"Hi babe," Kenzie said, her face suddenly breaking out in a wide smile.

"Oh my god, honey," Parker said, his face displaying alarm. "What happened to you?"

Kenzie quickly put her hand up to the left side of her face.

232

"Oh, I told about that," she said. "Jim hit me last night. That was the last straw that sent me away. This is just the first time you've seen it."

She had taken off the bandage before her shower. From below her left cheekbone up to her eye, the skin was several shades of blue and grey. In the middle of it was the cut from Jim's ring. After her shower, when she saw that there was no seepage from the cut, she left it uncovered.

"Holy shit, baby," Parker said, "I'm sure glad you left that bastard." He settled back on his love seat as Kenzie agreed with him. "So where are you?" he asked.

"I only made it to Kansas City," she replied. "I'm in a Motel 6. Getting out of Denver this morning took a while, and I didn't get much sleep last night. It's not as far as I had hoped to get today, but I didn't feel like I could keep driving tonight."

"That's okay. I'd rather have you safe."

"I looked at the map a little while ago, before my shower. I'm still about sixteen hours away, so it doesn't look like I'll get there tomorrow night."

"That's fine, babe. We'll have lunch together on Wednesday."

"I can't wait!" Kenzie said, smiling.

"I was happy to hear you were at a Motel 6," Parker said with a grin. "Means you're not too much of a snob. I'm afraid I don't have much to offer just yet."

Kenzie shook her head.

"I don't have a problem with frugality, and now I especially need to be careful with what money I have!" She tried to see over his shoulders. "So you're in your apartment now?"

"Oh, yeah," he replied. "It ain't much, but it'll be home for a while. Especially after you get here." Parker lifted his phone and slowly turned it, showing her his surroundings. By the time it turned back to his face, he saw the look on her face, and he smiled.

"Yes," Kenzie said, "it definitely needs a woman's touch. And some furniture!"

"Well, I got the bare minimum now. A love seat and a bed. Maybe we can go shopping for a few more things this weekend."

Kenzie smiled at the thought of actually sharing domestic life and responsibilities.

"God, I wish you were with me now!" she said, as her smile faded with her burgeoning sense of longing.

"I know, baby. I do too. But it won't be long. You've already whittled quite a bit off that 1,684 miles! I'm proud of you."

Her smile returned as she looked at him.

"I love you, Parker," she said.

"Aw, honey, I love you too!"

uesday morning, Hunter woke up early. Tense, and anxious to get the case files, he couldn't sleep. He had showered and shaved, and was on his first cup of coffee by seven o'clock.

But then he hit a standstill. He knew he probably wouldn't have the new files for at least a day or so. With Kathy's and Jenny Norbert's cases, any supposed leads he may have had were dry. He didn't know what to do with himself.

He was pacing, feeling restless, and he saw his laptop on the end table where he had left it. He had a thought and put his cup down on the coffee table. He sat down and woke up his computer. If R.J. was so burned out, maybe he hadn't put much effort into locating the killer's car, since he didn't have specific registration information.

Hunter logged back into the police department's web site, hoping that R.J. hadn't changed his password after their conversation yesterday. In just a few seconds, he was rewarded with the internal home page, complete with search entry window.

He clicked in the search box, then sat there watching the cursor blink. He was trying to think of what to search for. Finally, he just typed "Dodge Dart."

The database displayed a page with numerous police report summaries, many more than he cared to count, let alone read. And as he scrolled to the bottom of the page, the row of page number icons showed him that there were over a hundred such pages. Overwhelmed, he looked at the page for options.

He saw a "cross reference" button and clicked it. A second search box opened. Again, he sat and thought, casting about for ideas of what to search for, how to narrow the list. It surprised him that there were so many Dodge Dart references in police reports. But then he realized that the vast majority of these entries were probably older files that had been entered into the database, but dated back to when the Dart was still in production.

He didn't know the exact year of the car that Lily saw in the garage at Kathy's murder site. She said she thought mid-70s, but couldn't say for sure, and definitely couldn't pinpoint it. He thought about the time period of Kathy's murder and typed "2011" and hit "Enter."

That narrowed it down quite a bit, but still there were several pages. As he was scanning the summaries, he noticed references to "Durham," "Chapel Hill" and "Wake Forest," and he realized how to narrow it even more. The database was showing him a collective list of police reports in the region. He clicked "cross reference" again and entered "Raleigh."

That left three reports. Much better!

Hunter skimmed through them. He clicked the link for the first one and saw that it involved the theft of a tricked out 1970 Dodge Dart. Why anybody would have spent the money to embellish a Dart, as if it was some kind of muscle car, was beyond him. Even more confusing was somebody risking arrest and incarceration to steal it. The car was metallic green.

He closed that window and clicked on the link to the second file. It reported a citation for failure to stop at a stop sign. The car was a 1972 Dodge Dart, white. He closed the window.

Stopping just short of crossing his fingers, Hunter clicked the link to the third file. A 1975 Dodge Dart was involved in an accident in which a pedestrian was struck and killed. The date of the accident was Monday evening, September 5, 2011.

Labor Day, the date that Kathy was killed.

The car was brown.

Hunter's heart was pounding as he read the report. The driver of the car was a man named Jack Ferris. The officer who filed the report, Officer Greene, had actually witnessed the accident and stated that it was his opinion that Ferris meant to leave the scene before Greene pulled behind him, blocking his way.

Ferris was nearly in a panic, which Greene acknowledged was not that uncommon after such an incident. But when Ferris attempted to make a break on foot, Greene was forced to arrest him and place him in his patrol car.

Ferris was found guilty of vehicular manslaughter and served two years and five months of a three year sentence. The car was impounded, its contents itemized when the police did a routine search. The list was considerable as it had been packed, as if for moving. Just scanning through the list, something jumped out at Hunter: "Cutlery set in wooden box." Might not have raised any red flags for cops searching a packed car after a traffic accident, but in the context of Hunter's search now, the flags were waving desperately.

Hunter saw that Jack Ferris was released a month and a half ago, just days before Jenny Norbert was murdered.

Almost frantic, now, Hunter searched for any current information. He found a reference to Ferris' parole officer, and as he continued scanning, he found his last known address, in Northeast Raleigh.

He pulled out his phone and called R.J.

"Hey, Hunter," R.J. answered. "Calling for another favor?"

"Yeah, I want you to arrest a murderer!"

"What?"

"I found him!"

"You found who?"

"Who do you think? The killer!"

"What, just like that?"

Hunter exhaled loudly from exasperation.

"No, not just like that. I did some police work. I'll tell you all about it someday. The guy's name is Jack Ferris, and his most recent known address is in Northeast Raleigh." Hunter looked at the screen and dictated the address to him.

As he was talking to R.J., he got up from the love seat and gathered up his gun, his keys and a jacket.

"How did you find this?" R.J. asked.

"Don't worry about how I found it! You'll only get pissed at me. Just get some units over there and arrest the son of a bitch!"

"Okay, fine," R.J. said with a heavy sigh. "I'll head over there and check it out. But don't get your hopes up, man. I mean we've gone this long with absolutely nothing, not a single lead. And now suddenly you think you found the guy?"

"I don't think it, R.J. I know it! Now get your ass over there!"

"I'm going!" R.J. replied impatiently. "You want to make the bust? Wait, what am I saying? You're not a cop."

"Smartass," Hunter said. "I'm still at home in Allure, but I'll head down there." He looked at his watch and saw that it was just after eight o'clock. "This time of morning, though, it'll take me over a half hour to get there. Go get him, R.J.!"

"Alright. We'll be there in five."

Hunter rushed out the door and into his car. He sped out of his neighborhood, but then very quickly started chafing as he got on the main roads, and then onto the highway, and saw how slow and heavy the traffic was. Rush hour my ass, he thought. Now, he missed having the flashing lights and siren, having traffic part for him. Without thinking about it, he started scratching his wrists.

Hunter consoled himself with the thought that at least they'll get him, even if Hunter himself wasn't there to nab him.

Ten minutes later, R.J. called him.

"We missed him, Hunter. He's not here. Looks like he's cleared out."

"Shit!" Hunter pounded the steering wheel.

"He left a few things here," R.J. continued. "An ancient computer and printer, a couple of pots and pans, but there aren't any clothes or food here. You ought to see the wall over the computer, though. Looks like something out of that movie, *A Beautiful Mind*. You know, like some kind of crazy flow chart. We'll get pictures of it, but so far, it looks pretty indecipherable."

Hunter heard a voice in the background.

"Hold on, Hunter," R.J. said.

There was a pause with muffled talking. Then R.J. came back on, an unexpected urgency in his voice.

"Hunter, listen: One of the uniforms was looking at that chart on the wall. In all the mess, he found a name and address. Lily Sage. He has her address, Hunter!"

Kenzie felt the stare. She glanced up to her right and saw the man watching her. She felt a moment of panic, until she saw him smile and lift his coffee cup as a toast. She smiled briefly, then turned her attention back to her fruit and yogurt parfait. She tried to settle more in the shadows of her booth, with her laptop in front of her.

She had seen the café last night touting its breakfast and brunch specialties. When she saw they also offered free Wi-Fi, she decided to bring her computer with her.

"I think I'm about to get hit on," she typed.

"A guy there in the restaurant?" Parker replied.

She sensed a movement to her right, and in her peripheral vision, saw the man approach her. She glanced up just as he came around in front of her and he saw the bruising and the cut on the left side of her face. There was a moment of shock, she thought she recognized a flash of sympathy, followed by a quick look at his watch. He forced a quick smile and continued past, leaving the restaurant.

"Yup," she typed. "One look at the left side of my face and he was gone."

"Asshole!"

"Yeah, he should have followed through, swept me off my feet, huh?" she typed with a smile.

"You know what I mean, goofball." Kenzie's smile spread wider when she read his response.

"I won't keep you," she said. "I know you're about to leave for work."

"Yeah, just fixing to walk out the door."

"Well, I'm going to shoot for Huntington, WV. Then I'll just have a few hours to drive tomorrow."

"That's great, babe. And you got the directions I sent you for The Sawmill?"

"Yes, I did. Thank you. Looks very easy to find. I'm thinking I'll probably be there between noon and one o'clock."

"I'll be there! I'll be the one with my arms spread wide and my grin even wider!"

"I can't wait!"

"I love you, baby."

"I love you, too. Have a good day."

"You too, honey. Be careful."

Parker disconnected, feeling like an asshole himself. His afternoon with Marlys less than three days ago was still very much on his mind. Not that he wanted to continue a relationship with her. But the sex had been incredible!

He felt guilty keeping it from Kenzie, even though he knew it wouldn't accomplish anything to tell her. It's not as if they were even together, yet. Still, it would likely only hurt her as well.

I'll bet she's a hot little lover, he thought, hoping to replace the memories of Marlys with anticipation of making love to Kenzie.

So far, it hadn't been working. It also didn't help that he was still feeling guilty about leaving Lily. Especially the *way* he left her, with her knowing he had been unfaithful.

She looked more hurt, more vulnerable than he had ever seen her in the last three years. Leaving her in her current state of mind would have been bad enough, but with this added to it, he had never felt so contemptible.

242

He and Hunter hadn't spoken since Lily overheard their argument on Sunday night. He missed having his brother to talk to. He felt so alone

But at least, he'll finally be able to see Kenzie tomorrow!

With a sigh, he picked up his keys and left his apartment.

Kenzie got in her car, anxious to get on the road again. She skimmed the directions she had printed at JuleighAnn's from Google Maps. I-70 to St. Louis, then onto I-64 the rest of the way into Huntington, West Virginia. Piece of cake!

She pulled out of the parking lot and up the ramp to the highway. With her sunglasses on and her visor down, she began the day's journey into the sun.

Jack Ferris parked his rusty brown 1975 Dodge Dart under the carport, next to Lily's Corolla. It wasn't much concealment, but it was better than parking on the street. He looked around, then pulled the black spandex hood over his head. He was already wearing his Edward Scissorhands suit. A pair of latex gloves finished off his ensemble.

He picked up the wooden box and a flat pry bar from the seat next to him, opened the door and got out, pressing the door closed quietly. He walked cautiously around the front of Lily's car, staying as hidden from the street as possible and constantly keeping a lookout down the driveway. He didn't like the openness of the carport.

He probably should have taken care of Lily last night, under cover of darkness. But after it had gotten dark, Jack was busy packing his belongings into his car. The whole time, he was listening to his internal advisors about the best way and time to do it, but they couldn't agree. He was getting mixed messages. The voices made him tired and he just went to bed.

But in half an hour, he'd be on his way out of town. He wanted to leave Raleigh, North Carolina far behind him.

At the door, he tried the knob, but it was locked. It was an older house, and he was hoping for some wear and tear. He pressed his shoulder against the door, testing it. He felt it give a little against the pressure. He slipped the bent end of the flat bar between the door and the jamb, just above the knob. He pulled firmly, while holding the knob. It didn't take much. He was pleased with the results. It didn't even make much noise.

Once inside, he placed the flat bar on the kitchen counter. He pulled the pistol out of his pocket and proceeded quietly through the kitchen and into the dining room. He was starting to feel afraid that he had missed her somehow, when he heard a soft shuffling a couple of rooms away, like papers or magazines being moved around.

He turned a corner to his right, crossed a hallway, and came into a cozy family room. And there she was, straightening a stack of magazines on the coffee table. The phone rang, and when Lily looked up to get it, she saw him. She froze, her eyes wide and staring.

He was pointing the gun at her, but she didn't even look at it. She was focused on the hood, on his featureless face. The phone rang about six times, then stopped. Less than a minute later, it started ringing again. Lily didn't seem to notice.

"Come in here," he said quietly, motioning toward the dining room.

Frozen in place, barely breathing, she didn't move. He walked toward her, around the side and then behind her, and through it all, she still didn't move. He pressed the gun against her back and she jumped. A little more pressure and he propelled her forward.

This one is going to be easy! She's not even putting up a fight.

By the time they made it into the dining room, though, she was shaking, shivering as if she were cold.

"Get on the table," he instructed.

She shook her head almost imperceptibly. Pressing the muzzle of the gun against the back of her skull, he pushed her forward against the table.

"Get on the table," he repeated, his voice soft yet firm.

Lily leaned over the table, wishing he would pull the trigger, wanting finally to be free of the pain, yet afraid to provoke him. She squeezed her eyes closed tightly against the tears that were coming.

"Shit!" Hunter hissed as he punched the red disconnect button on his phone.

He had already gotten turned around, heading back now toward Allure, almost causing an accident in the process. But traffic was heavy at this hour. Weaving in and out of openings, ignoring the almost continuous blaring of horns, he was in a near panic. A long stretch of shoulder was coming up on the right, and he worked his way over there, accelerating once he was out of the traffic.

He thumbed Lily's number again, listening to the rings, until their voicemail greeting began. She hadn't returned his previous two calls, so he didn't bother to leave another message.

A few hundred yards ahead, the shoulder narrowed for an overpass. Hunter knew he had to get off the shoulder, but the traffic was almost bumper to bumper. He leaned on his horn, as he rushed past, moving slightly to his left toward the traffic. He was fast approaching the concrete abutment at the beginning of the overpass.

Drivers heard and saw him coming, and out of self-defense, inched to the left, often returning fire with their own horns. By now, Hunter was going slower than he would have liked, but still the abutment rushed past on his right, leaving barely enough room for the film of dust on the side of his car.

The shoulder widened again after the overpass, and he made up some time then. His exit was coming up ahead and he sped past those in the exit lane, accompanied again by angry honks.

Once he was off the highway, traffic was lighter, but there was still the danger of slower local traffic and pedestrians. He sped as quickly as he dared, without a siren or lights, toward his destination.

Lily was dazed. Once she was on the table, Jack had struck her with the butt of the pistol. He didn't need her fighting him as he was attaching the zip ties. He opened the hinged wooden box, the one that Monica had brought home all those years ago, and which contained the scalpel that ultimately proved to be her undoing.

The box had been packed in his car, along with almost everything else he had owned, when he had been involved in the accident. When he got out of prison, everything seemed to have been thrown in the vehicle, not packed neatly as he had done, so he knew the police had gone through the contents of the car. He had been extremely relieved that the box of knives had not raised any warnings with them.

The knives and scalpels were still fitted in their spaces, but Jack had also added a collection of zip ties. He selected a long one to go around the table leg, and he left quite a bit of slack in it. He selected a shorter one and, inserting it through the loop of the previous one, wrapped it tightly around Lily's wrist. He followed suit with her other wrist and her ankles, and finished just as she started stirring again.

As Lily came to and realized her predicament, she struggled, crying. *Now* she could fight back, she thought in her panic, when it wouldn't do any good, remembering her lethargy a few minutes before.

Jack ignored her struggles, her whimpers and cries, and focused on his memories. Remembering how the dining room table had always been Sonya's place for punishing him, having him lean over the table and grab onto the edges, while she paddled his butt. He thought it was only fitting that the dining room table now be used as *his* place for administering punishment.

"It will be over soon," Jack said quietly as he knelt down to select a knife from the box.

Chilled by his calm voice, Lily continued struggling, and she felt the table start wobbling. She remembered the loose parts under the table, the leaf sliders that had come apart and the apron that was mostly detached. It was that one job that seemed to continually be moved to the bottom of Parker's to do list.

She wrestled mightily against the zip ties until she felt something collapse. What happened next took place in only a couple of seconds. The table legs that her ankles were attached to tipped over to the side, and that end of the table crashed to the floor. The impact caused the leaf sliders to come apart, and the table ended up in its two halves.

Jack was alerted to the noise of splintering wood and looked up toward the table just as it collapsed. Instinctively he reached for it as a piece of the apron, torqued by the impact, split and impaled his left hand. He yelled in pain as he stood up, blood pouring out of his hand.

As the table crashed down, Lily hit the back of her head hard against it, wincing under the new pain. She was aware of the killer behind her, and of something warm and sticky dripping down her face, but as she slipped again into unconsciousness, she thought she heard another sound from the direction of the kitchen.

Hunter pulled his car to a stop behind the old Dodge Dart and ran to the side door. His Glock 22 in his right hand, he moved quickly but quietly as he pushed the door open into the kitchen, and he saw a bit of the broken door jamb on the floor. He also saw the flat bar on the counter and recognized how Jack Ferris had gotten in.

A few more steps and he saw, through the doorway into the dining room, the splintered dining room table, with Lily tied to it, her head and face covered with blood. Feeling the breath go out of him, he knew he was too late. Lily was dead.

He had been too slow to find the killer, and now another woman he loved had paid with her life. Feeling the despair drop over him like a shroud, he crossed the threshold into the dining room. In the moment he saw her bloody body, he was already drenched in a depression deeper than any he had felt in the last three years.

He wasn't aware that Jack was waiting on the other side of the doorway. Jack swung the length of the broken piece of table apron and struck Hunter's wrist, knocking the Glock out of his hand and slamming him back through the doorway.

Hunter backed into the kitchen, watching this strange figure in front of him, wearing an outfit of old black leather, festooned with zippers and buckles, and a black hood with zippered openings for the eyes and mouth. He remembered Lily's description of a man with no face.

Jack had dropped the piece of wood and took his pistol in his right hand, pointing it at Hunter, his left hand still dripping blood. Hunter had backed up as far as he could go, against the kitchen counter. Jack continued until the gun was only a couple of feet away from Hunter's head.

Awash in anguish and misery, Hunter closed his eyes and felt the tears roll down his cheeks. He knew now that no amount of scratching would ease the itching he felt in his wrists. If only he had been able to finish the job back then.

No more pain!

He just needed to go to sleep and it would all be gone. One bullet is all it would take. He started willing Jack to pull the trigger and put him out of his misery. He opened his eyes again to look at Jack, and when he did, he saw a movement beyond him.

Lily was stirring, and while her wrists were still immobilized, she could move her legs around, since those table legs had broken free. The sound of her movement distracted Jack, who turned slightly.

The realization struck Hunter in an instant – Lily was alive. And she needed him! That moment of Jack's distraction was all Hunter needed. Gripping the flat pry bar on the counter behind him, he swung it at Jack. Jack was just turning back toward Hunter when the bent end of the bar crashed into his head, the claw embedding itself almost three inches into his skull.

He collapsed on the kitchen floor, a dark puddle forming around his head.

Hunter stepped over him and rushed back into the dining room.

"Are you alright, hon?" he asked frantically as he knelt down beside Lily.

She seemed confused as she looked at Hunter. Beyond him, in the kitchen, she saw the body of the killer, and she knew it was over. She looked back at Hunter and nodded.

Hunter reached across Lily, took one of the knives from the box and cut the zip ties from her wrists and ankles. Once she was free, she threw her arms around Hunter, buried her face in his neck and cried.

Still kneeling beside her, Hunter held her tightly, his elation bewildering in the face of the despair he had felt just moments before. As they heard a distant siren approaching, Lily sat back against the half of the table top that was still resting diagonally on two legs.

They both felt exhausted, physically and emotionally, but they felt relieved that it was all over.

"I guess Parker can scratch this table off his to do list," Hunter said.

A black Silverado extended cab pickup raced northward through North Raleigh. It was shortly after 9:00 a.m. and traffic was thinning out a little, so it was able to make good time.

At the sign pointing the way to Raleigh Memorial Medical Center's emergency room, the truck took a hard right, the rear tires scratching sideways a little on the pavement. There was a small parking lot, but a few spaces were open. The pickup skidded to a stop in one of them.

Parker burst out of the truck and dashed toward the glass doors. He had to pause since the sensor didn't open them as quickly as he wanted them to. Once inside, he ran to the desk.

"Lily Sage?" he said breathlessly.

The nurse glanced at her computer screen, then pointed.

"Exam 3, right down there, in the corner," she said. As Parker ran off in that direction, the nurse's eyes followed him down the hall.

Parker paused. The door to the room was ajar. It was a small room, packed with medical equipment but not much in the way of aesthetic comforts. There was a bed that was little more than an examining table, and Lily was on it, with a sheet pulled up to her waist.

A chair had been pulled to the side of the bed, and Hunter was sitting there, holding her hand. Parker stood there for a moment until Lily glanced up and saw him.

"Parker," she said softly.

Hunter turned and stood up.

"Hey, little brother," he said. "Come on in."

Parker walked tentatively into the room.

"It's okay, Boo," Hunter continued, seeing his hesitation. "She's going to be fine. She has a concussion and they want to watch her for a couple of hours, but she'll probably be able to go home tonight."

Parker looked from Lily to Hunter and back again, but had yet to say anything. Hunter put a hand on his back and guided him toward the chair.

"I'll let you two talk," he said, then he left the room.

Parker looked at Lily for a moment.

"So, I hear we have a dead body on our floor," he finally said. Then he corrected himself. "Or, *your* floor."

Lily smiled weakly, but then she shuddered a little.

"Yeah, Hunter killed him."

"You smiled!" Parker exclaimed.

"I've been known to do that," Lily said, raising her eyebrows a little.

"I haven't seen it in a long time. You're so pretty when you smile. I've missed that."

"Well," Lily replied, looking around the ER exam room, "despite all this, and two knots on my head, I feel pretty good today."

"You mean you're better now?"

"No, not like you mean. I'm still an emotional and psychological mess. That'll still be an issue for some time. I'm sure I'll still have to see Jane for a while. And I still miss Kathy terribly." Her eyes filled with tears when she mentioned Kathy. "But I do feel better. Hunter was saying that getting the killer might give us both closure, so I don't know, maybe that's it."

Parker nodded and was quiet for a moment.

"So," he finally said nervously, "you and Hunter?" His voice trailed off at the end.

"Me and Hunter?" Lily echoed, confused, raising her eyebrows.

"You're together?"

"No," she said, the confused expression intensifying. "Why would you think that?"

Parker started feeling stupid as he thought about his reasons.

"You just seemed to start getting better when you were with him. And just a few minutes ago, you were holding his hand."

Lily looked at Parker through narrowed eyes.

"Good lord, Parker," she said, her voice reflecting amazement, "that's quite a jump you made there. Is that why you took up with those other women, because you thought I was getting it on with Hunter?"

Parker felt his face flush and he looked down.

"Hunter was holding my hand to comfort me," Lily continued. "I've had a little bit of a stressful morning. And as for starting to get better, it wasn't just because I was with him. It was because he helped me to start remembering things. I started feeling useful. Maybe it's related to that whole closure idea. I don't know. But no, dummy, I'm not with Hunter."

"What about me?" Parker asked as he looked back up at her.

"What *about* you?"

"Do you want to be with me again?"

"No," she replied. Parker inexplicably felt tears forming. Whether Lily noticed them or not, he wasn't sure, but she continued. "I mean not yet. You hurt me, Parker. You hurt me bad. I'm not going to just get over that. That's going to take time. I mean I know I wasn't easy to handle, but I'm your wife! What happened to 'in sickness and in health'?"

Parker remembered mentioning that clause just a few weeks ago when talking to Hunter.

"I know. I'm so sorry," he said, but he felt the first glimmer of hope he had experienced in relation to Lily in a while. "But you think there's a chance?"

"Who knows, Parker?" she replied. "If you can keep your dick in your pants when you're around other women, maybe."

Parker sighed and one of those tears rolled down his cheek.

Kenzie threw the drapes open, illuminating the little motel room. It wasn't much of a room, but she liked the location, and it had a great view.

She had arrived at her target destination, Huntington, West Virginia, at about five o'clock. She knew that just a little ways beyond Huntington, her eastward journey turned south, at Charleston, so she decided to drive another hour or so. She found the little family-run motel south of Charleston, tucked between Interstate 64 and the Kanawha River. The sign faced the highway to attract travelers, but the rooms, wisely, were situated toward the river.

Beyond the wide, slow-moving watercourse, past a complex of rental storage units, Kenzie looked at the forested hills, stretching out for miles. The view reminded her a little of the foothills of Colorado.

And just five hours to the south was Parker! They were in the same time zone now. She smiled and turned away from the window.

She sat down at the table and looked at the little binder of guest information. Shuffling through it, she found a page that contained instructions for accessing the motel's Wi-Fi, and she opened up her computer. She pulled up Facebook and went to her ongoing personal message conversation with Parker.

"Hi baby," she typed. "I made it to Charleston, WV. Only five hours away. I can't wait to see you tomorrow!"

She sent another message, this one to JuleighAnn, letting her know she was alright. Then she spent some time checking her notifications.

By seven o'clock, she still hadn't received a response from Parker, though it showed that he had seen her message shortly after she sent it.

Must be busy, she thought.

She decided to go out and get some dinner.

Parker felt his phone buzz, but he ignored it as he finished signing the papers. Lily was being released and Parker was taking care of the paperwork. He had spent the day in the emergency room, watching doctors and nurses examine the bumps on Lily's head, looking into her eyes, and there was even a visit from a hospital psychiatrist to see how she was dealing with the trauma she had endured.

Parker wasn't looking forward to the statement from his insurance company, but he was glad he had it. Hunter had driven Lily to the hospital, so at least the insurance didn't have to cover an ambulance ride.

The clerk was a rather hefty woman in her forties with a soft, pretty face. The name tag pinned just above her ample left breast proclaimed that her name was Lois. She picked up one stack of papers and painstakingly lined them up, tapping them on her desk, then pounded a staple through the corner. She handed the stack to Parker and smiled.

"Okay, Mr. Sage. You're good to go."

"Thank you, Lois," Parker said, and he picked up the papers and stood up. As he walked away, Lois surreptitiously kept her eyes on him, noting how his t-shirt clung to all his delicious bulges, watching the curve of his butt in his tight jeans.

As he turned a corner, and walked out of her view, Lois sighed and turned her attention back to her paperwork.

Parker fished his phone out of his pocket. The icon showed that he had a private message from Kenzie. God! In the last several hours, he had all but forgotten about Kenzie. Rather than continuing toward Lily's exam room, he stopped in the hallway, to read Kenzie's message. She was five hours away and looking forward to seeing him for lunch tomorrow.

Shit! How could he have been so stupid? How had he let himself get into this situation? He stared at Kenzie's message, debating how to respond. Nothing was coming to mind.

When he saw a nurse pushing Lily toward him in a wheel chair, he closed Facebook and put his phone away.

Parker drove slowly toward home, being overly cautious for Lily's sake. He didn't want to risk any kind of injury or upset.

"Parker, I'm fine. It's okay to do the speed limit," she said.

"Sorry," he replied, and he sped up just a little.

When they finally arrived at the house, Parker pulled into his spot under the carport. Curiously, Hunter's Impala was parked behind Lily's Corolla. Lily noted that the killer's car had been taken away.

Parker got out and went around to help Lily out of the truck. It was after eight o'clock in the evening, getting dark and chilly, and Lily was tired. She was usually in bed before now.

As Lily got out, she looked toward the door of the house, dreading what was on the other side, on the kitchen floor. Before they got to the door, though, the light came on and Hunter opened the door.

"How you doing, Lily?" he asked.

"I'll be fine, Hunter. Thanks." Her face was set into rigid lines as she stepped up into the kitchen. "What are you doing here?"

Then she saw the kitchen floor. It was clean.

"I was able to talk the police into expediting their investigation here, and then moving the main focus of it over to Jack Ferris' apartment. I didn't want you to have to come home to a bloody crime scene."

"Well, bless your heart, Hunter." As Parker closed the door behind them, Lily looked at where the door jamb had been broken. "You fixed the door, too!"

"I'm not without skills," he replied with a smile.

They passed through the dining room where the pieces of the broken table were stacked against the wall. There were some dark, wet spots on the carpet. Hunter looked up at Parker with a devious grin.

"I didn't know if you wanted to add 'reassemble dining room table' to your to do list, little brother. So I left it here in case you did."

"Thanks, Hunt," Parker replied. "You're all heart."

"Yeah, and Lily already blessed it." He pointed at the spots on the carpet. "There was some blood on the carpet here, but it's being kind of stubborn coming out."

"I don't know," Parker said, "I'm thinking that maybe it's time to see if we got hardwood under that carpet."

When they came around the corner into the family room, they saw that Hunter had a fire going in the fireplace. Parker got Lily settled on the sofa and was glad to see that she was visibly relaxed.

"Well, listen guys," Hunter said, "I'll be going now. Lily, I'm glad you're feeling better."

"Thank you so much, Hunter," Lily replied. She shook her head. "That sounds so inadequate considering you saved my life!"

For a moment, Hunter remembered how close he was to letting Jack Ferris put a bullet in his head. Before he realized that Lily was alive and needed him.

"I kind of think we saved each other," he said quietly.

"Thanks, Hunt," Parker said. "I'll talk to you later."

Hunter nodded and left.

A few awkward moments passed between Parker and Lily before Parker spoke.

"I guess you're probably pretty tired," he said.

"Yeah," Lily nodded, closing her eyes. "I need to get to bed."

"Well," Parker pressed on nervously, "if you want, I could stay."

Lily opened her eyes and looked at Parker.

"Don't worry," he continued. "I'll sleep out here on the sofa."

Lily looked away, remembering the hurt he had caused her. Then she remembered how close she had come to being murdered. She thought for a few moments.

"I think that might help," she finally said.

Kenzie stared at the screen of her laptop. She had sent another message to Parker before she went to bed last night, telling him goodnight and that she loved him, as she usually did. And this morning, there was still no response.

She had a bad feeling.

"Parker," she typed, "is everything alright? I hope nothing bad has happened, and that you're just busy. Or maybe you broke your phone."

Possible scenarios started going through her head.

"But then you still have a computer, right?"

A couple of weeks ago, it had occurred to her that if anything happened to one of them, the other one might never know. They only had one mutual friend in Facebook, and he wasn't someone either of them knew personally. The only way they might have even an inkling that something was wrong was if one of them just stopped making contact.

But he had seen the private messages she sent last night.

"Parker, I really hope you're alright. This isn't like you."

Thoughts came unbidden into her mind, a number of possible incidents that could prevent him from making contact. An accident on a construction site, a car accident, or perhaps she had said or done something to piss him off. She scrolled back through their conversations over the last couple of days. She couldn't find anything that might have caused offense.

"Have I done something to upset you?"

She sighed. This was apparently a waste of time. It was seven o'clock. She decided not to have breakfast at a restaurant. That would take too much time. Instead, she would stop at McDonald's and eat something on the way.

"Parker, I'm leaving now. I'll be at The Sawmill at noon. Please be there. I love you!"

She wiped away a tear and closed her computer.

There was a chill in the morning air as Parker sat on the edge of his front porch, his face displaying the confusion and anguish that he felt. His elbows on his knees, he leaned his head against his left hand. His right hand held his phone to his ear.

"You're home for the day, huh?" Hunter asked him.

"Yeah, I told the guys I wanted to stay with Lily. They can handle what's going on today."

"So Lily took you back?"

"Not really. Not yet, anyway. I slept on the sofa. But I didn't want to leave her alone today."

"Probably a good idea."

"Hunter, I'm sorry about the way I was acting Sunday night. I was stupid."

"Yeah, you were." Hunter paused for a couple of seconds. "But I was a little off base, too. I know you've been dealing with some heavy shit. So I apologize, too. I should have remembered that you weren't blessed with my intelligence and level-headedness."

"You're an asshole," Parker said, giving in to a slight grin.

"Yes, I am, little brother."

"Kenzie's on her way."

There was silence for a few seconds.

"I'm sorry, what was that?"

"Kenzie left her husband. She's on her way here now. I'm supposed to meet her at The Sawmill at noon."

"So," Hunter said, the sarcastic edge returning to his voice, "you're demonstrating once again your lack of intelligence and level-headedness?"

"Don't start with me, man. Up until you called me yesterday morning, I really thought I wanted to be with Kenzie. I didn't realize I still loved Lily until I almost lost her."

"I thought you were so in love with Kenzie."

"I am. I mean I've heard it ain't possible to really be in love with two different people at the same time. But I do love Kenzie. And I do love Lily."

"Well, little brother, my advice is the same as it has been for the last few weeks. You need to make a decision. You're going to have to pick one."

"I have. Kenzie's wonderful, and like I said, I love her. But I've loved Lily since I first laid eyes on her. I know what I had with her, and for the first time in three years, it feels like I have a chance at getting that back. I belong here with my wife."

"So what are you going to do?"

"I don't know," Parker replied with a heavy sigh. "Kenzie's going to be devastated. She doesn't have a place to stay, she doesn't have any money, she doesn't know anybody here except me, and I'm letting her down."

"Just tell her the truth. Women are stronger than we give them credit for. Just look at Lily."

"I'm afraid to go there."

"You're afraid? Look, Parker, when I said women are strong, I didn't mean that Kenzie might beat you up."

"That's not what I'm talking about," Parker replied. He thought about how to put his fear into words, but he couldn't think of a way that didn't make him sound stupid or weak.

"Well," Hunter said, "What is it, then?"

"I'm afraid if I go there and see her, I'll do something stupid and fuck up my chances with Lily again."

It was Hunter's turn to sigh.

"I don't know how you got along without me the last couple of days."

Kenzie sat at a table near the front door of The Sawmill. It was just a few minutes after noon, and there were a few people having lunch. She sat alone, intently watching whenever someone came in the door. She had already told the waitress she would wait to order until her friend arrived.

She hadn't had any way to check and see if Parker had ever responded. She felt so alone and disconnected without her phone.

She was tense, but she didn't realize it was obvious until the waitress touched her on the shoulder and Kenzie jumped.

"Hon, are you alright?" the waitress asked. "Is there anything I can get you?" She placed a glass of water down in front of Kenzie.

Only then did Kenzie realize that her hand was pressed tightly against her chest. She forced herself to relax and to take a deep breath.

"No, thank you," she said with an attempted smile. "Just the water for now." She took a long drink as the waitress nodded and walked away.

All morning, during the entire drive here, she was racking her brain, trying to figure out what could have happened to Parker, why he hadn't responded to her messages.

The only thing that seemed to fit was her worst fear, something she didn't want to think about. A fatal accident was her worst case scenario. Otherwise, he would have found some way to contact her.

Logically, she knew she had absolutely no evidence of such an outcome, that she was jumping to conclusions based entirely on conjecture. But emotionally, she was a wreck, with that one possibility taking hold in her brain.

The door opened, and someone came in. It wasn't Parker, though. Just another good old boy coming in for lunch, she thought. Then she felt a little ashamed at that description, remembering her earlier prejudice against the south.

She closed her eyes and took another deep breath, slowly letting it out. She opened her eyes when she heard the door open again, and again, she was disappointed. It was a good looking man, but it wasn't Parker.

Oddly, though, he was looking at her and walking directly toward her.

"Kenzie?" he asked.

She nodded nervously.

"I'm Hunter Sage, Parker's brother. Do you mind if I sit down?"

She shook her head, still nervous and intrigued.

"You're the detective," she said, remembering her conversations with Parker.

"Yes ma'am, I am."

He sat down in front of her, and as he did, the waitress approached.

"Hey, Hunter," she said. "What can I get you?"

"Nothing right now, thanks," he replied.

"I didn't know you were waiting for Hunter," she said to Kenzie. "He's one of our favorites."

Hunter gave an embarrassed smile as she walked away, then he turned back to Kenzie. He looked at her for a moment as he took a deep breath.

"Kenzie, I'm afraid this is kind of awkward. But my brother's not coming."

Kenzie could feel the tears welling up. She didn't know what the problem was, but it didn't sound good.

"He said he'd told you about his wife, Lily, and how she witnessed the murder of my wife three years ago"

"Yes, he did," Kenzie said quietly. "I'm so sorry."

"Thank you. Well, yesterday, the murderer came after Lily. He almost killed her, but I killed him first."

"Oh my God!" Kenzie said.

Hunter closed his eyes and shook his head. Kenzie noticed that he seemed nervous too.

"This is all just my very bumbling way of letting you know that, having almost lost her, Parker realized that he still loves his wife."

Kenzie closed her eyes, forcing the tears out and down her cheeks.

What a dumb, naïve idiot she had been. If only she had listened to JuleighAnn! Now, here she was 1,684 miles away from anybody she knew. And without a job. With basically only a few dollars left, she was little more than a vagrant.

How could she have been so stupid?

Hunter looked at Kenzie, at the tears that streaked her cheeks, and wished desperately that he could do something. And that nasty bruise and cut on her cheek. Parker had told him that she was in a bad marriage. Did her husband do that? Hunter couldn't imagine doing that to a woman.

But God! She was so pretty! That long, incredible red hair. Those warm brown eyes. And from what he had seen so far, she had a sweet disposition, despite these difficult circumstances. He could certainly see why Parker had fallen for her.

"Anyway," he said, trying to salvage his explanation, to make her feel better, "I volunteered to come and let you know."

"Why didn't Parker come?" Kenzie asked.

"Well, ma'am," Hunter said, and he took a deep breath in preparation, "the thing is, while he loves his wife, he loves you too. He wanted me to be sure and tell you that. And he was afraid that if he came here and saw you, spent any time with you, he might lose his resolve."

He stared at her for a moment, absorbing her face, her expression. "Frankly," he continued, "being here with you now, I think I can say for sure he most definitely would have wimped out."

Kenzie looked at Hunter for a moment, apparently unsure of how to respond. The sadness seemed to give way to anger.

"I left everything I knew and drove all the way out here, because Parker said he loved me and wanted to be with me. So now, here I am, half a country away from my home, with no job, no place to live, and no money."

"Yeah, I know," Hunter said as he fidgeted in his seat. "That is certainly a less than ideal situation."

"Less than ideal?" Kenzie said with raised eyebrows, as she angrily wiped a fresh tear away from her eye. "Yes, I would say that this is definitely less than ideal!"

"He feels really bad about that, and wants to make it up to you. Which is why we kind of worked out an arrangement for you, if you're interested." Hunter took a deep breath as he saw Kenzie's eyes narrow. This wasn't coming out very well. What the hell was wrong with him? "Parker just got a new apartment a couple of days ago," he continued. "Turns out he's not going to be using it, so you're welcome to it."

"Great! I have an apartment. What am I supposed to pay for it with?"

"The rent's paid through the end of October. After that, since he feels like a real shithead for convincing you to come out here, and frankly I agree with him, he'll continue to pay the rent until you find a job, another apartment of your choosing, or decide to go back to Colorado."

Kenzie looked at Hunter, her eyes still narrowed, her mouth open slightly. He wished he knew what she was thinking, but he was afraid to ask.

He decided to take a different tack.

"Don't decide right this minute," he said. "You're probably hungry. Why don't I buy you some lunch, and we can get to know each other. You'll be able to think about it a lot better on a full stomach."

The burgers and the beer did help. Enough, at least, that Kenzie's anger had eased, and was giving way to the sadness again. But even the sadness, she noticed, wasn't as keen as it had been. She was relaxing. She wasn't okay with what had happened to her life by any means. What she had done to it. But she was gradually coming to terms with it.

She knew that dumping her life and moving cross-country to a new, unfamiliar place was phenomenally dumb. Doing so without money or a job was even dumber. And to the south, of all places, an area that had never attracted her. In fact, this entire episode was probably one of the dumbest things she had ever done in her life.

But she realized that she was free now. Free from an abusive husband. Free to change the course of her life, at least to the extent that her upcoming employment and financial circumstances would allow. She was free to do what she wanted to do. And it was Parker who had given her that courage.

This realization helped her, little by little, to accept her new situation.

So did two beers.

And so did Hunter's personality. His sarcastic and sometimes self-deprecating humor, reminded her a little of Arden, back in Colorado. She felt comfortable with him, and she sympathized with the difficult job he had taken on, of coming here to break the news to her about Parker. As their third beer arrived, Kenzie was feeling at ease.

"So," she said with a smile, "have you always cleaned up your brother's messes?"

"Pretty much," Hunter nodded. "I'm much better suited to that than he is. He got the looks and I got the brains."

"Oh, I think you got more than just brains." Kenzie's face flushed a little when she realized that she had actually said that out loud.

"Well, I know I ain't as hunky as Parker. It's been a few years since I've had a six pack anyplace other than in the fridge."

Kenzie smiled. She wanted to say that she thought he was *very* attractive, but she managed to stop herself. He did have a certain hardness to him that Parker didn't possess, but it all softened up whenever he smiled.

And with her, he seemed to smile quite a bit.

Damn! What was it about these Sage boys?

"Um," Hunter said hesitantly, looking at her face, "did your husband do that to you?"

Kenzie self-consciously put her hand up to her face and nodded.

"My husband is a really cold, angry, jealous, conceited, self-important douche bag." She smiled when she finally got to the end of the list, and Hunter returned the smile.

"No wonder you married him! I can certainly understand the attraction," he said.

"Yeah, well people sometimes change over time. We were both young and immature when we got married. As we grew up, we both changed. I became the sweet demure person you see sitting before you, and he became an asshole."

Hunter tilted his head in a sort of shrug.

"It happens." He looked at her face for a moment, at her warm brown eyes glowing in the light from the front windows. "I'm

272

glad you got away from him. Even if it didn't turn out quite like you had hoped."

She returned his gaze for a few moments, comforted by the warmth she felt from him.

"I am too," she replied, with a somewhat confused look on her face. "Even though I'm broke and homeless and without any visible means of support, I'm oddly glad I came."

"Well, about that," Hunter said, "have you had a chance to think about the offer I made?" Kenzie delayed for a moment by taking a sip of beer.

She thought for a moment longer, then looked up at Hunter. "It feels suspiciously like being a 'kept woman,' but at the moment, I don't really see that I have any alternative."

"Good!" Hunter said. Then he quickly backpedaled. "I mean I'm not glad you don't have any alternative, but I'm glad you're staying."

He made a face as if he were exasperated with himself for his clumsy statement, and he took a drink of his beer. Despite the scary position Kenzie was in, she couldn't help smiling at Hunter.

As they had eaten their lunch, The Sawmill had quieted down as patrons went back to work after lunch. Now as it was getting noisy again, Hunter looked around, noticing all the people. He looked at his watch.

"Damn, girl! We sat here all afternoon. It's almost four o'clock."

"No wonder my butt's asleep!" Kenzie said.

"What do you say? You want to go out and walk it off?"

"Even for me," Kenzie smiled, "three beers in four hours isn't that much to have to walk off. But yes, I'd like to walk around."

"Good." Hunter reached in his jacket and pulled out his wallet. He took out bills that he knew would cover their food and drinks, as well as a generous tip, and left them under his glass.

"Shall we?" he asked as they stood up, and he helped her put her jacket on.

Kenzie felt him lightly place his hand on the small of her back as he opened the door and guided her out, and she smiled. Once outside in the cool air and the quiet, they stood for a moment, each stretching their backs. Then Hunter looked down at Kenzie. She looked back, wondering what was on his mind.

"What?" she finally asked.

He grinned, apparently nervous again.

"I know we just had lunch, but I was wondering if I might be able to take you to dinner."

"Yeah," she replied with a smile, "I'd like that." Digging a fist in a sore muscle in her back, she continued. "Do you know of any place where we can eat standing up?"

www.ingramcontent.com/pod-product-compliance
Lightning Source LLC
Chambersburg PA
CBHW020046180626
46812CB00010B/471